The Waymaker

The Library of Congress has cataloged as follows:
Palmer, Rod
The Waymaker / by Rod Palmer
1, Mimms, Ameena (Fictitious character) – Fiction. 2. Christian Fiction – Huntsville – AL
Case no. 1-8065989681

ISBN: 978-1-7339633-4-3

The Waymaker

by Rod Palmer

Black Wren Press
Columbia, SC

Refusing to forgive requires
the tedious upkeep of hatred.

~ Betty Palmer ~   DV Survivor

The Waymaker

THE RUDE AWAKENING

THREE robbers sit in a tinted Cutlass, stewing outside of New Birth Baptist Church of Huntsville, Alabama. Their sighs can't soothe their nerves. The job is easy, it would seem. They have guns; prayer is the only weapon of sheep. It's their shepherd, God, that worries the thieves. The money might be cursed in their hands.

The driver digs masks out of a paper bag and hands them out. Old School, the front passenger with a sawed-off pump in his lap, holds the mask up and studies the red, collapsed rubber face with punched out eyes. He smirks at the irony. "Devil masks bro?"

In the backseat, New York nervously rolls his toothpick over his tongue. "I don't kill on Sunday's B. And I ain't trying to get caught up in no murder case neever, so y'all keep them guns pointed at the ceiling, ya feel me?"

The driver, Scoop, has a cherished secret. The collection plate robbery is nothing compared to what he alone stands to gain, but in order to collect his windfall he must first make New Birth's first lady a widow.

Old School checks his watch. They must account for an extra collection plate going around for Bishop Simon L. Bonneau's birthday love offering, which will be applied to his private jet fund. Ever since the bishop attended the African American Pastors Summit at the White House, he came out of it politically motivated, but also obsessed with getting himself a private jet.

Simon's highly criticized White House visit left such a wide philosophical rift in New Birth's leadership that Simon feared a coup, which makes New Birth the perfect target; the robbers can count on a slow moving investigation from all the potential suspects on the inside – as long as the robbery goes smoothly and they don't kill anyone.

The robbers, playing it by ear, waiting for the band and choir to fade down, which would signal that the money has been bussed up to the front and consolidated for the taking, and the ambush would begin with every unsuspecting eye shut in prayer, blessing an offering the church would never claim.

The music, however, isn't fading; it's growing. Emanating from that domed castle of a building is the full-bodied praise of the white-robed, Simon L. Bonneau Choir, their unified voice trumpeting:

There is power
In the name of Jesus
To break every chain
Break every chain
Break every chain

The Holy Ghost pops like popcorn in the sanctuary. The band and choir let the spirit take the wheel. In that auburn carpeted sanctuary, arms waive in praise and tears stream down the faces of many worshipers; many who have had chains broken; many still draped in chains yet to be broken.

Their shepherd, Bishop Simon Bonneau, sits cross-legged, marveling at his flock, shaking a fist while shaking his head, his black dyed hair greased over his balding cul-de-sac.

A worldly eye sees the brass buckets being filled by a congregation of many that struggle with bills and debt, yet unwittingly extend themselves further to ensure that a man, already wealthy beyond their comprehension, will never again have to fly commercial. Financial sacrifice, however, is the prerogative of the giver and their God. Their praise is not for the man who sits in the most magnificent chair in the building; true praise is for God. True praise is personal.

Those who praise the fiercest, often convulsing with the Holy Ghost, have been through the most. The young lady with red-rimmed glasses and shoulder-length hair, coming toward the altar with her arms raised in surrender, had been stabbed eight times and left for dead by her, then, boy-friend's other girlfriend. A stocky man in a navy-blue suit and salt and pepper afro hops in place as if on a pogo stick because he is the living after-photo of the fidgeting heroin addict he once was.

Praise looks back to the past. Looking back over their life and seeing the wretch they used to be versus the tes-timony they've become – seeing the hell they'd been through versus the glory they now bask in; seeing the horri-fying alternate endings where they could've been dead and gone, or somewhere drooling in a mental hospital, versus the miracle that they are – first and foremost – still here. Children of God whoop, holler and dance because they see God's grace realized in the steepness of the arc of their ver-sus; this is the frequency upon which the Holy Ghost flows.

Not one among them, however, has a more complicated relationship between present and past than Ameena Mimms, who stands at the left end of the middle row, with a frenzy of natural, curly hair flaming out of a head wrap that's blue like a robin's egg. Ameena's dark family secret from a long ago past made her flee to New York at an early age, where she found her calling in theatre. That same dark secret made Ameena abandon her acting career not long after ascending to Broadway and even receiving a Tony award.

Ameena weeps with chains draped all over her; she sings, There is power in the name of Jesus/ To break every chain/ Break every chain/ Break every chain. Although Ameena sang musicals for the last decade, her voice kept its old hymnal soul. The reason Ameena left Broadway has everything to do with the young lady praising next to her, Rose, who is wearing the most convincing wig that Ameena could afford her.

A year ago, Ameena was standing at the balcony of a high-rise apartment, when her mother called with Rose's diagnosis. Ameena had answered the phone giggling because there was a shirtless man (whose name she cannot recall) standing behind her, kissing her bare shoulder, but then she had heard her mother say, through the phone, that Rose was diagnosed with cancer. Ameena's phone dropped, and along with it, the fabulous life she had become accustomed to. The following day, Ameena was back in Huntsville at her mother's dining room table, staring at her ghost reflection in the glass China cabinet with no China. It's been a year. Treatment showed promise in the beginning, but overall has been a very slow fail. Just recently, they learned that Rose's cancer had progressed to terminal. By the joy in Rose's praise, though, no one could tell that she'd received a death sentence. She, too, sings, *There's an army rising up/ There's an army rising up/ To break every chain/ Break every chain/ Break every chain.* So mature, now, in her short Christian walk, Rose's praise is no campaign for healing, but a praise of gratefulness; knowing how God will strengthen her spirit, if not her body.

As the song fades, Willie Dantzler, a New Birth associate pastor, is returning from the restroom. Speaking of pasts, Will was a gang banger, according to many who knew the old him. A person from Will's past is out there in the parking lot, getting out of the passenger seat of that Cutlass wearing a devil mask, and coming towards the building; it's Old School, the middle member of the trench-coat-wearing demonic triplets, now trotting toward the building like Navy Seals on an extraction mission.

Will can't beat the offertory prayer back to his seat, so he stops and readies for the prayer. He discovers, late, that he had stopped right next to Ameena: Miss Attitude – which makes her beauty an unforgiving tease. Regardless, Will steals a look, verifying that the beauty he holds in his mind isn't touched up by boyish fantasy. Again, he sees how her face wears a magazine shine, the way her maple forehead drains light down along the nose bridge, which pools at the curve of her cheeks. Her shocking white teeth sparkle, in concert, with the glassiness of her brown eyes – this beauty, animated with the grace of a seasoned thespian. She makes a living on stage; even her contemplative pause is bottled drama. Will has never felt more simplified in the presence of any woman. His heart breaks when he considers what could have been.

Ameena's praise pipes down and she notices the last person she wants next to her, Willie (Ameena refuses to call him Will for short). "Good morning Willie," she says, but not without vandalizing the name, making it ten times more country than it is: Wheelie.

Will turns weary. "For the life of me, I don't know what I done to you, Ameena," Will grumbles. "Do you even know?"

She knows. Without a shadow of a doubt, she knows. Being with this man would connect her to the shame that she now lives to forget; it would bear the torch of one generational cycle that Ameena is determined to break. Yes, Ameena knows the reason, but it's not the reason she gives. "Sometimes people's spirits just don't agree – and they don't have to. I'm fine with that."

Not to be outdone, Will says, "Are you sure that's what it is? Or maybe you think Broadway done took the stink out-chya boo-boo. Next time you get up from a good number two, turn around and take you a long whiff."

Ameena's face sours at a smirking Will. She replies, "That, sir, would be the only thing that you and I have in common."

Will huffs. "Crazy… I used to wonder why you was single. Not no mo."

A hush descends over the congregation. Willie focuses forward and finds himself in the high beams of first lady's blue contacts. Bianca is behind the pulpit, poised for the offertory prayer, but perturbed, as if she can't bless the offering until Will and Ameena's chatting ceases.

Bianca is a different woman from the thirty-year-old South Carolinian who, a decade ago, dropped onto New Birth's scene out of nowhere, scandalously rushing to the altar with the recently widowed Bishop, a man twenty years her senior. Bianca has since dyed her hair blonde and bleached her skin, perhaps for fear of falling out of favor with her color-struck husband and her in-laws. There are bets out that in another five, ten years, Bianca would be certified Caucasian. Her mind's eye makes her a queen gazing out over her subjects; she is born for this. Bianca clears her throat to convey that what she will say has some gravity to it and requires her to take her time. Since rushing to the altar with the bishop, she no longer rushes for anything anymore, now believing that her crown, her reign, as New Birth's first lady is as secure as the earth beneath her feet. But then she spots three devils trotting in through the entrances.

At first, there's only a few scattered screams because it seems, for a moment, like the prowling devils might've been a badly timed and distasteful praise dance ensemble, but mayhem breaks loose when an automatic weapon belts like a construction jackhammer indoors, making snow fall from the ceiling.

Folks flail and run and trip and fall. The devils contain the chaos with pointed guns, shouting threats – pure foxes in a henhouse. More shots ring out. "Get back!" Says one devil. "Sit the fuck down!" This, he says in the sanctuary of God, as casually as if it were some night club. The devil on the right calls out the head deacon who was hiding behind the cart of money. "You! Get up! Get up!" Slowly, Deacon Smiley stands, palms raised, forehead wrinkled with worry.

The masked man barks out instructions and whacks the deacon with his gun. The deacon drops, but hurriedly, crawls to the collection trays and begin dumping them into a burlap sack provided by the robber. New Birth is a budding mega church, so the collection plates are many.

First lady is down. She'd fainted since the first shot. Her feet sticks out from behind the podium, the toes of her red high heels pointing upward, as if she were flattened by a flying house. The congregation crouches under the pews, crying out, chanting prayers, babies wailing, as if holed up in a storm shelter at the height of a howling hurricane. All the while, Bishop Simon Bonneau stands tall like an oak tree defying the storm. He browbeats one pistol-toting devil who then rotates his stiff gun-arm like a clock-hand that lands on Simon. Scoop says, "What, old man… You think your God can save you now?"

Simon comes down the auburn steps like he's bullet proof. He stops one step from floor level and says, "Ye though I walk through the valley in the shadow of death, I shall fear no evil for thou art with me –"

"– Are you sure? Are you sure He with you?" Scoop's

head nods aggressively; the gun hand tightens. "It's time this money help somebody other than you."

Bishop is unnervingly calm with his reply, "And who's somebody? You?"

"What I'm doing right now, ain't no different than what you do every Sunday."

"I don't have to hide behind a mask," Bishop Simon goads.

"You ain't nothin! You ain't walked through no valley, but I'm 'bout to put you in the shadow of death, right about now. God art with me, bruh," says the devil, through immovable, rubber lips. One of the other robbers notices the altercation and yells, Money's over here bro. That's all that matters!

"God's with you?" Bishop laughs. "All terrorists think they're carrying out the mandate of God. If you don't know the voice of God, you have no idea what voice has taken up in that head of yours, son."

It seems, to the congregation, that bishop is getting through to the masked robber, but out of all the words the bishop spoke, only one word struck Scoop like an arrow and made his gun-arm slacken noticeably. That word was son.

Bishop steps down again, reaching floor level, his hand out for the gun, saying, "This is not God's way. I can guide you to the light if only you would put down the gun, son."

"No!" Scoop takes a half step back, his aim stiffening again. New York and Old School are yelling. *Yo! What are you doing, man!*

Bishop stares down the gun barrel and says, "That money can't buy you what you truly seek. Salvation is free; it is right here for you to claim." Bishop is aware of the sanctuary cameras recording the service. If he could embrace the gunman, let him feel God's ready acceptance through him, the video would inspire millions. Bishop eases closer, peering into the mask's eyeholes to see if murder is in the gunman's eyes, but bishop sees something else. Bishop stops, snake-bitten by the recognition of eyes that he hasn't seen up close in thirty years. In the liquid of those familiar eyes, bishop sees a small, glassy memory from a long time ago, about equal in years of the gunman's age. Small in the cornea, of the gunman's eyes, Bishop Simon sees a young lady curled up on the bed, crying, and he sees himself standing in the hotel room, buttoning his cuff links; that vision curved to the roundness of those eyes identifies the gunman. Bishop remembers seeing that same woman from the hotel sitting in church a few years later with a son who was a few years old. That son is this gunman.

The shot hits bishop like a face punch. The back of his head spits a red plume and he drops. Shrill screams rip the atmosphere. The other robbers check. They agonize over Scoop's error. Bishop lay at the altar, as still as a cut tree; a neat, dime-sized hole in his forehead, his eyes open, frozen in the recognition of his illegitimate son.

Members, after seeing their pastor shot down like a dog, and remembering the Charleston Nine church massacre, they think better to chance escape than rely on the mercy of gunmen. People rocket up from under the pews, lifting like a carpet of heads. They rush like rapids down the aisles, bottlenecking at the exits. In the rushing tide of people, at least three stand frozen: a robber pointing his gun at Ameena and Rose.

Will dives between the gunman and the women, shielding them as he says, "You'll have to kill *me* first!"

The red devil in steel toe boots raises the gun to Will's head, now preferring him.

Will's arms spread, ready for ascension. "There is a place already prepared for me." Tears spill from his eyes, leaving glistening tracks down his face. He fully believes he'll be walking on a floor of clouds, directly, but mourns the thought of leaving without goodbyes to the people he loves. Will says, "You pull that trigger, you send me to paradise, but you're sending yourself to a lake of fire."

Old School doesn't dare say a word for fear of his voice giving away his identity. He lowers the gun and runs to catch up to the other two.

Once the robbers are out of the sanctuary, people begin sprouting out of hiding, out from under pews and tables, from behind instruments, from the nooks between open doors and the wall. They're peering out of doorways and standing at the glass panes with cupped hands to see if the coast is clear. They check for loved ones, check their own bodies for injury. Many are on frantic 911 calls; the reality hitting afresh during the telling. All the while, Ameena and Rose cling to each other, weeping within the enclosure of Will's broad wingspan, Ameena regretting every cross word she's ever said to the man. She can't thank Will enough. Ameena needs more time, more life to get her affairs in order.

Will hangs with them during the sorting of the chaos and helps account for the missing. Mrs. Bethune sits upright, her whole long pew empty but for her. There is no music, but she trembles as if tapping her foot to a song, her mouth shut tight, her left arm shrunken against her body. One person calls for a wallet for Mother Bethune's mouth; she is suffering a stroke.

Will hangs close by until cameras arrive. He looks up, the sun on his face as he follows the overhead passing of a helicopter. Will darts off, saying he'll be back. Cell phones stream the broadcast, where members see, on national broadcast, what they're seeing with their own eyes but with a bottom banner that reads *Active Shooter, Huntsville, AL*.

A gathering forms around a reporter. Interviewees take their turns, tearful and scattered. They call for Ameena, the only member to be singled out by a gunman and live to tell about it. Before taking off to join them, Ameena checks for Will, the man she wants recognized for being her hero, but he's nowhere in sight. With Rose in tow, Ameena shoulders through the crowd, en route to the reporter, her head on a swivel, still scanning for the man who stands a head above the crowd, Will, but he is nowhere to be found.

DEN OF THIEVES

An hour later, the robbers are at the hideout, an off-road, rusted, singlewide trailer now overrun with vines; a former trap house, abandoned even by dope fiends. A rank mattress stands upright against a wall, shafts of sunlight beam through rot holes in the ceiling. All masks are off. The loot still not divided because the robbers are embroiled in an argument.

Old School stands between Scoop and New York, begging them to chill.

New York yelled, "How am I'm supposed to chill, dawg? Thanks to ya mans, here, this about to be a murder investigation! Do you know what that means?" He pauses, allowing a few beats of the vessel thumping at his temple before answering his own question. "They investigate murder way different, B. They'll stop at nothing!"

Scoop leans into his words. "So, I guess all that yellin's finna undo what's already been done, huh…"

"This lil bastard think this is a game," New York yells.

Scoop replies, "*I* shot the nigga, not you!"

"In the eyes of the law we all shot him. Ain't no such thing as an accessory to murder in a strong-armed robbery, bruh. We was s'pposed to go up in that church, get the dough, and be out," New York yells. "But nah, you had to go have a chat with the bishop? Now, because of you, I got a *murder* hanging over this money, bruh!" New York pops his toothpick back in his mouth and walks away, fuming.

He stops in front of the table of money and sighs.

At the exact moment that New York sets down his gun, two gunshots bang in his ear and hammers his chest, jarring him senseless. The toothpick falls from his lips. With a nod, New York looks down, confirming two holes set apart like eyes, crying deep red blood down the front of his white shirt – crying for all the wrongs he can never right. His ears ring like windchimes. Hot slugs fry in his body. His head raises, leveling with the horizon, the eyes widen to get a good look at death, looming like a thick fog. His final image of the mortal world is of the two men that shot him, their guns now turned on each other in a standoff.

New York's two shooters hear him collapse. They hear him wheezing, but neither sees; they can't afford to take their eyes off each other's gun.

Old School and Scoop hold their aims on one another, each stunned by the unlikelihood of not only independently planning on turn their two accomplices into ghosts, also putting it into action at the exact moment. Now they're at a standoff, each pointing a gun, each staring down the barrel of the other's, death now but a finger-twitch.

Calm, yet determined, Old School says, "I'm gettin' *all* this money, ya hear. I'll die for it."

The younger man's left cheek pulls a half smile from his lips. "Have the money," says Scoop. "I don't need it."

"If you don't need it, why you shoot New York, huh? If you don't need it, why's yo gun pointed at me?"

"I'm the trigger man. Either of you might give me up to the cops for a reduced sentence. I can't let nobody mess this up for me. Not even God."

Old School warns, "If you don't go over there and get me my money, I'll have you standing before God, directly, so you can take it up with Him in person."

Scoop smirks. "I thought you would've seen the resemblance by now."

Old School's head raises a clip, his eyes squinting. "You killed your own *daddy*, boy?"

"I'm getting in on the inheritance. The loot is yours. This has got to be a good – what, thirty, forty racks, over there? All yours."

"So, we gon' lower these guns or what," asks Old School.

They're sweating. Both men – careful not to be duped – study each other as they released the gun clips and eject their chamber rounds. They sigh, exhausted from the suspense, the world around them now awakening. They now hear the rustle of rats, the birds chirping outside, a woodpecker's hollow Morse code echoing in the forest around this lone rusty trailer.

Scoop asks, "Who was that lady, though?"

"What lady?"

"I'm not doing this with you, Old School. You *know* who I'm talking about. Shawty was kinda dark skinned, natural hair, makeup done real nice… Fine as a mug, to be honest witchya."

Old School swats the conversation. "You stupid if you don't know who that was. She's an actress. I just wanted to get a look up close."

"You didn't seem starstruck to me." Scoop says. "How would you know what I seemed like, under that mask?"

"See, I'm thinking you know her. Just like I rolled up on Simon just to see myself in him, I think you were doing the same thing. If she recognized you just like my sperm-donor of a daddy recognized me, we done for."

"I don't know her and she don't know me, bruh. So, you can go-head on wit dat."

Old School goes over to the money before minds change, before guns are reloaded. He goes to the living room where the floor is swollen in the middle, the boards shifty under the moldy carpet. He stands over New York, respectfully.

"Good ole Keyshawn," Scoop says, from the kitchen. "Where do you suppose we hide him?"

Old School replies, "He already hid. Don't nobody come back here." Old School picks up Keshawn's loaded gun off the table, weighs it in his palm. He then aims at Scoop who is now unarmed, his life flashing before his eyes in the dry-rot kitchen. Old School laughs, and then lowers the gun. Scoop palms his chest and gasps. "Yooo… Don't freakin' play like that, man."

Old School chuckles as he empties the gun. He asks, "The family know about you?"

"I didn't find out he was my pops until I was like twenty-two. Missed out on *all* eighteen years of child support. A long time ago, I approached the daughter – my half-sister. Booshy broad spit in my face."

Old School sighs and says, "You could've had a whole different life. Pops could've afforded you a top-notch lawyer, got you off with probation. You coulda had yourself an education – everything. Now here it is, you done did six years in the belly, now damn near homeless, laying wit some broad in her section-eight pad with huh four head o' children? C'mon now."

The dead bishop's son says, "Moms was too ashamed. She was married, but she and the man I always thought was my father had been on and off during those years. They were living apart when I was conceived. Ma dealt with so much. I put her through so much. Now I'm finally fixin' to give her the life she should've had a long time ago."

"Well, you better hurry because if they divide that estate before you contest it, it could be held up in court for years."

"You ain't saying nothing but a word, bro. I'll be talking to first lady even before the wake. If she wanna reject me like the daughter did, they all can talk to my lawyer for all I care."

"Have you thought about your *other* inheritance, young-in'?"

Scoop's lips tighten. "I know ain't trying to talk about my momma."

Old School's eyes slice in ridicule. "Listen at yo dumb butt. I'm talkin' bout the other-*other* inheritance: I'm talking about the kingdom of God."

Scoop gives a resounding *bruh*, his arm unfurling like a magician's viola, presenting the stolen church money and the dead man – evidence to just how hypocritical is Old School's talk of religion.

Old School sighs and shakes his head. "You better start thinking about repentance before you find yourself standing unprepared before Him," he says as he hoists a bag over his shoulder. With a sole owner, the money no longer needs dividing, so they take the sacks and leave a motionless New York lying in the abandoned trailer.
Old School leads down a bushy half mile path that leads to a dirt road just as long.

Scoop, trailing a few steps behind, asks, "So, you gonna tell me who you work for?"

"Who I *work* for?"

"When you laid out the plan, you said you ain't never stepped foot in the church, but how'd you know there was going to be an extra collection plate or the time the money's collected and which entrance and hallways would get us in there unseen?"

Old School keeps on tramping through the high bush, saying nothing.

"You said you was gon' take all the money, right? But there was enough there for each man to get broke off. See, I'm thinking maybe you want it all because you gotta split it with whoever cased the joint for you." Again, Old School doesn't respond. Scoop probes again. "Actin' all surprised when you found out who I was… I think you recruited me on purpose."

"I let you in on it because you was my cellie, remember? If I had a different cellie, I would've had a different partner."

Quietly, Scoops shakes his head. "Crazy. Like, what are the chances?" Scoop swings the sack of money from one shoulder to the other. He scans left and right, confused. They've gotten so far that he could no longer see the trailer, New York's rusted, ratty tomb. "Are you sure we're still on the path?"

Old School looks back with a stern cut in his eyes. "Do you *ever* shut up, man?"

"I mean, this path is mighty overgrown don't you think? I really don't see a lane cutting through; just bush."

"You don't see the path because you' lookin' down. Look yonder to the horizon where the trees open up in the distance. You on the path, whether you know it or not."

They walk a while in silence, swatting gnats, hearing only breathing and the breaking of twigs underfoot. Scoop asks, "So, I guess you not gonna tell me who you working for huh?"

Old School would leave the question unanswered. He shades his eyes from the sun, remembering one of Bishop Simon's last statements, *All terrorists think they're carrying out the mandate of God.*

HANGING ON

Charmaine is – first and foremost – grateful that pictures of Ameena and Rose are not all she has left of them. They are still there, peopling her home – still, thankfully, getting on her nerves, with Rose so charmed by that luminous, tablet thing in her lap that she won't much lift her eyes when spoken to. All day Charmaine had spontaneous fits of weeping. Stopping in front of a wall picture, vacuum in hand, and while sprinkling seasoning in a rolling pot, just thinking about what she nearly lost had made storms rumble in her bosom, made her face kink with spasms that turned her ugly and shy. People make you feel, Charmaine would say; if you don't got nobody, then you ain't got nothing to feel but empty. Charmaine stirs her cooking pot, but the pot isn't all she's stirring. "And wouldn't you know," Charmaine dares, finally, the shame finger stiff as a rod. "… the *same* convicted felon you was settin' up there judging, turned out to be the hero that saved your life."

Ameena looks up from setting the dinner table, hearing, finally, what she had expected to hear from her mother. "An I-told-you-so just hours after I had a gun in my face? You are so wise, ma – if that's what you need to hear." Charmaine's head lay back. "Don't worry 'bout me. What you need to do is thank God and shut ya mouth."

"I am grateful for what Will did, ma, but only that gunman knows if Will actually saved my life or not."

"Child, you got a talent for making simple things complicated, you know that?"

"And *you* got a talent for making complicated things simple."

Charmaine huffs. She sprinkles a little salt. She stirs and sips from a tasting spoon, her eyes stuck on Ameena, wondering how a creature like that came from her, being so poised, and dry – and judgmental to top it off. "You let that good man go, just to prove a point. Careful that's how you end up in life: *right* but alone."

"Can we not do this, ma?"

Charmaine echoes her own words, "Right, but alone."

"Will and I were never together anyway. We were only friends."

"Child, ain't no such a thing as a man friend that tall and fine, hear me?"

Ameena studies Charmaine from the corner of her eye. "Ma, spare me please."

"Spare me please," the mother mocks. "Think 'cause you speak proper, you speak smart, huh…" She turns the pot lid face down, head shaking, her indictment, a two-word song, "Jussa dumb…"

Will feels undeserving of Ameena's gratitude. He didn't *decide* to jump in front of the gun; he'd acted without conscience. But since Ameena's gratitude comes with an invitation to a home cooked meal, he couldn't refuse. Ameena was apologetic over the phone when she told Will that dinner was only neck bones, collard greens and cornbread, but it sounded like lobster and caviar to the bachelor who normally eats from take-out boxes, or from a pot of spaghetti – the one meal he knows how to prepare.

Ameena and her mother, Charmaine, thank Will from the doorway to the dining room where Rose sits, eating already. Rose couldn't wait on their guest. She cannot take her last round of medication on an empty stomach.

Rose eats quietly, watching the adults interact, as if she's watching a bad TV show. Will's heroic act had affected her differently. He didn't save her life. No man could, says doctors. Will gave her months; months more of suffering. Rose asks to be excused, awaiting Charmaine's nod before leaving.

"Not feeling well," Ameena informs a curious looking Will.

Will replies, "Sorry to hear. Think, maybe, it's that stomach virus going around?"

"– No –"

"– Yes –"

"– It's nothing."

Ameena and Charmaine smother the concern so hurriedly, Will can't tell who said what. He *could* tell, however, that the topic of Rose's health is off limits.

Ameena quickly changes the subject. "Crazy how Bishop's still alive isn't it?"

Smugly, Charmaine adds, "And they say God don't make mistakes."

"Ma!" Ameena periscopes to her mother who shrugs and then shovels a fork of collards into her naughty mouth.

"He might not be dead," Will begins. "But he ain't alive, either. I went down to I.C.U earlier and got a look at him through the glass. It looks bad. Heck, mother Bethune isn't doing too good either."

Ameena frowns. "Mother Ida Bethune… I saw her on a gurney. What happened to her?"

"Stroke," says Will. "The gunshots, the crowd… Must've been too much for her. As for Bishop, they got him on a ventilator, wrapped up like a mummy. They don't know yet if he can breathe without the aid of the machine. The *only* person talking like Bishop's bout to get up out that hospital bed to preach come Sunday, is First Lady."

"Makes perfect sense," says Ameena.

"Are you kidding me," Will says, from the side of a packed cheek. "How do you figure he's preaching Sunday when they was picking up fragments of his skull off the altar? He'll be a zombie of himself, at best."

Ameena's fingertips rap the table until Will is finished. Wisely, Ameena says, "I was not referring to Simon. I was referring to Bianca – how it makes perfect sense that she won't accept his death. She worships the man like he's God Himself, so how is Bianca – in her mind – supposed to reconcile the death of God?"

Will raises one brow, "Is that shade? I thought you and first lady was tight."

"We *were*. Until I had seen enough."

Will's head dips. "Enough what?"

"I don't want to be mean," Ameena cancels, as she sits up straight and resolute, as if refusing her food along with the question, but then on second thought, Ameena squints and says, "Here's the thing about Bianca: Bianca's wealth affords her the ability to live outside of reality. The church house, to her, is nothing more than a big dollhouse. But that's just me, talking. I'm sure Bianca has something negative to say about me as well."

"Like?"

"I feel like I disappointed her. She expected me to come down from Manhattan acting like some sort of champagne-sipping celebrity, bringing a certain level of attention to her circle and to her little showy events, but I wasn't about to be a name drop for Bianca and her cackling friends."

"Amen," Will adds.

Charmaine sprouts a smirk. "I bet I can tell ya who's gonna take Bishop Simon's place."

Who, asked the other two, Will's *who* seeming defensive.

Charmaine eyes Will like a con at a poker table. "Now's *not* the time to be bashful, Willie. You gon' mess around and let Javon Saunders jump in front of you."

In shock, Will's eyes flutter like they're stinging. "But he *is* in front of me. That man's been tarrying for how long now? He's fifty years old. I'm thirty-four."

Charmaine points her fork at his insolence, saying, "Javon ain't what New Birth need. In him, I see greed, ambition; he'll be Simon Bonneau all over again. But you?

You're approachable, you're 'umble – walking around looking like you work for the business you own. Plus, you and that motorcycle gang –"

"– Bike club."

"– What's the name again?"

"The Holy Roaders."

"Whatever…" Charmaine dangles a limp hand. "Y'all not shut up in the church; y'all out in the community, heppin' folk." The limp hand then extends its pointer finger. "And if a church ain't for the community it's for only a few. It's gotta be you, Will. You'll give New Birth the makeover it needs – with your big, fine, motorcycle ridin' self," Charmaine says, and then suggestively slurps a neckbone.

Ameena rolls her eyes. "Cut it out, ma."

Charmaine argues, "Hell, you act like *you* don't want 'em…" But then Charmaine swats her own comment. "Y'all know I'm just teasin' about that part. But seriously, Will, you need to shove on up to the front. We need you, brother."

Will's smile warps with modesty. "Thank you, mam. Dinner's excellent by the way."

Charmaine gets up to go. "I'm gonna go check on Rose," her excuse for setting the stage for this couple to be alone together. Charmaine pat Ameena's shoulder as she leaves.

Ameena and Will are alone like old times – old times being just six months – although they'd never shared a dinner table before this. Will wipes his hands and says, "Didn't know your moms was a cougar. How old is she?"

"She just turned sixty. Why? You thinking 'bout it?"

Will dismisses with a wiggling hand, his eyes squinting on a deeper concern. "Rose is fifteen. So, your moms was, like, forty-five when she had her?"

Ameena shrugs. "It happens."

"Obviously," Will settles, again sensing a landmine around the topic of Rose. He then switches his focus to something that makes him smile. "Look at you," he says.

On cue, Ameena tilts and bats her lashes, a hand patting the plush of her hair, kidding with the man she traded insults with that morning in church.

Mischief cut a smirk in Will's cheek, but any flirtation would seem like he's using his heroic act as a bargaining chip.

"Strange isn't it? Me and you at the same table," says Ameena. "I made a vow to be nice to you from now on. So, how am I doing so far?"

"Great," he replies. He then glances at Ameena's plate and giggles, "I'm not trying to be funny or nothing, but… Until now, I couldn't see the illustrious Ameena Mimms sitting in front of a plate neckbones."

"Ma cooks on Sundays," Ameena says. "Neckbones isn't really my thing."

"I see… trying to eat it with a fork as if you don't know no better." Will's giggle sounds forced and lonesome.

"Will," says Ameena, her face clear of humor. "Thank you. Thank you so much. I've been nothing but mean to you and you… doing what you did… putting yourself in harm's way like that…"

Will's eyes thin as if on a dare when he says, "You weren't mean to me *always*. We were friends not long ago. Remember our conversations?"

Friends would be the non-presumptive term, though neither had ever had a "friend" of the opposite sex where they'd linger hours after bible study, talking well into the night while the church parking lot slowly dripped empty. Ameena gazes momentarily, remembering those blissful nights, the pair leaning against her Beamer, eyes full of night stars while debating bible study topics, their affections coded under the guise of scripture.

"I remember our conversations," Ameena seconds. "But our conversations were always about the bible; not about us."

Will poses side-eyed. "Not *all* of our conversations were about the bible." Certainly not their last starlit conversation where Will had asked the question that had been puzzling him ever since Ameena's celebrated return to Huntsville.

"How are you not taken," he had asked.

Ameena blushed at the compliment his question implied. "I've been 'taken' much of my adult life; I'm just not taken right now."

"By choice?"

"Life suddenly got complicated. I certainly didn't leave Manhattan in favor of Huntsville's chitterling circuit," she had said, in lazy-eyed sarcasm.

"It's because of Rose isn't it," Will finally dared to ask.

Ameena had looked away, saying, "Don't guess, Will. For now, this one's for God only."

"Ameena, do you not feel safe with me? I find myself walking away from our talks wondering what I could have done different to get you to open up to me."

"You're good, Will. I'm certainly not critiquing you, in my mind, so don't do it to yourself."

"Maybe I can help you with whatever this problem is – you ever thought about that?"

"You're so kind, Will, but no thank you."

"Remember... even Esther, as queen of Persia, had to ask, in order to have her people spared."

"Esther?" Ameena was delightfully puzzled. "I'm trying to figure out if you're calling me beautiful or prideful."

Will replied, "What if it's both that makes you so captivating to me?"

Ameena looked down to hide her blushing. "You say the darndest things, William," she kidded. She was under the assumption, still, that Will was short for William. He never thought to correct her; he liked having a name that only Ameena called him. Ameena continued, "Thing is, the issues I got going on right now consumes every emotional resource I have to offer a significant other. If I were to plow a relationship through this mess? On the other side of it, I would find myself in serious emotional debt.

I've done that before and I won't do it again. I just hope that if the man that God wants for me, comes along, that that man would be patient." The way she smiled, and the way her eyes dipped, was a dramatic clue.

"Patient," Will confirmed.

Ameena had then dangled her car keys and said, "On that note…" They had parted ways for the night.

Now months later, sitting at the dinner table together, Will is dying to ask what had happened months ago, why the following Sunday after their hint of a relationship, did Ameena march past him as if he were a statue. Will looks across the table at Ameena, but she isn't looking outward; her eyes are open but looking inward. Perhaps she too toils with what could have been, or maybe she wonders what still could be. "Ameena?"

"Yes?"

"Are you okay?"

"I'm shaken, still, by what happened. The nerves won't leave me. Feels like radio static in my spirit. And I keep seeing it, those devils. I keep seeing the back of bishop's head turned to meat, but if you're asking if I'm saddened by what happened to our great bishop? That would be a hearty hell no. He got back what he put into the universe. No more no less."

"Strong words," says Will. "If you think bishop's deserving of being shot in the face, that makes me ask the question: What'd he do to you?"

"Nothing."

Will leans in, resting his elbows on the table. "'Nothing' must've happened on the same day I found you walking along the highway, upset."

"What're you – investigating his murder?"

"I *been* investigating him."

"What can you do to him now? He's all but dead."

"I know, for a fact, Ameena, that you were getting help

from the church."

"And that's exactly the reason why I hesitated to *ask* the church, because I knew my business would be out in the street."

"Your business is not 'out in the street,' Ameena. *I* know because I'm in leadership. I do know that it's something very sensitive because your paperwork went straight to Roxy."

Ameena can hardly hear him over the chatter in her own head. "I must seem like such a failure," Ameena sulks. "Everyone thinks I'm supposed to be rich."

Will's hand splays out on the table. "Yes or no, Ameena. Your sister has cancer, am I right?"

Two, three emotions pass through her like ghosts. Ameena clutches her belly, her brows tinged. "Say what?"

"Maybe no one had the heart to tell you that a kid wearing a wig is a dead giveaway."

"The wig," Ameena gasps abhorrently. It's not being outted that rocks her, it's learning that she was never hiding; the epiphany hits like a child learning that their shut eyes' darkness doesn't hide them from the world, but only blinds them in it. Ameena and Will join hands over the table. "It is cancer," Ameena confirms. She feels a tickle of relief that Rose's sickness is the *only* thing Will knows for sure. "Things got harder when Bishop Simon cut off assistance for so many. He put a private jet ahead of people."

"I was not in support of that, by the way," Will says, officially.

"You don't have to tell me that, Will; I know."

Will remembers being floored the Sunday Bishop announced the three-month limit to assistance, asserting, in a whooping, veined-neck indictment, *If ya need help mo then three months... You not going* through *something; you* are *the something. Don't like it? Find another church home. Be a burden on them!* Will shudders from the memory of the spirited standing-ovation bishop received from people of Christ. "He acts like the money's his –"

"– I went to bishop personally. I thought, maybe if he could hear, directly from me, what I was going through, he'd make an exception, but I couldn't get face to face with him. He is well guarded by his staff."

"Did you *ever* speak to him alone?" Will turns slightly, shielding himself from the horror he expects to hear, knowing what he now knows about Bishop Simon preying on women.

Ameena's hands fidget in her lap. She begins tearing up. "Yes. He said, if my little sister's life depended on his help, I quote, 'she gon be one dead little bitch – waitin on me.'"

Will turns ill. "Oh God."

Ameena weeps and shakes.

Will let go of her hands to hurry around the table where he sits by Ameena, consoling her.

Ameena's eyes shut tight to try to squeeze out the image of that day, but the back of her eyelids become a movie screen where she sees herself alone with the bishop in the lounge of his mansion, his house coat open, his chest melted with age and snow fallen with gray hair. He held a glass of golden port wine from the top, his ring finger tapping a rhythm on the glass rim. *Touch the hem of my robe*, he had said. Ameena snaps out of it, wondering if her face brought forth the disgust of that memory.

"Are you telling me everything, Ameena? I thought, for sure, you was fixin' to tell me that bishop tried to take advantage of you."

"No."

Will doesn't trust her response; it's too quick, too finite.

"Ameena, if he did, you're not the first. Me and some other leaders were trying to use his abuse of women to try to force him out. And when I say that there're many… I'm talking, like, twelve women, probably even more."

"Well, he didn't take advantage of *me* so," Ameena shrugs. "And for the record? I would think better of what you're doing for those women, if this was *before* bishop's trip to Washington – I'm just saying."

"I would have, had I *known* prior. We didn't go searching for a reason to oust the bishop; the women, all independently, started coming to us."

"There you go," Ameena goads. "Blame them."

"I blame *us* for having an environment where the women coming forward didn't think their justice mattered to us until it served a different agenda."

Without a rebuttal, Ameena starts cleaning the table, meticulously picking up everything she could, so not to waste her trip to the kitchen. She isn't gone long, but when she returns, Will is standing, as if signaling his departure.

Ameena asks, "Did I offend you?"

The leap of his brow shows how far from his mind was any thoughts of being offended. "No. Not at all."

"I cleared the table because it needed to be done, it wasn't a hint, Will." The truth is, being that the man who shoved a gun in her face is still on the loose, Ameena feels safer with Will there, but she can't bring herself to ask him to stay.

"No hint taken." He smiles fondly. "Sunday coming is a fifth Sunday. I still haven't finished my sermon."

"Oh…" Her lips shrink to a point, her hands gather in front. "Ok." Ameena ushers Will to the door but wouldn't let him off the front steps without, once again, expressing her gratitude. She leans into what she wants to say but the words vanish. She takes Will's hand. She feels him glitch, which alerts her to how badly this could go if she overstepped, so she retreats, emotionally, posting a smile as a coverup. Will notes her hesitation and thinks it could have very well been a cancelled kiss. Ameena's thumbs caress his knuckles, the air between them as dramatic as the sky, with its horizon bursting a chemical orange that gleams against smoky clouds, as if dragons had been warring above. Ameena's upward glance and her – *Beautiful isn't it* – prompts a discussion that lingers for a half hour.

They discuss the shooting, the questions it blows wide open. "Still no leads," exclaims Ameena, while scrolling through her phone.

"No leads because they looking outside the church. If they take a look inside, they'll find plenty folks who wanted bishop gone."

"Really? Inside, huh…" Ameena says. "Will? At the church, when the police and the news vans showed up. Where were you? Everyone was looking for the hero." Ameena realizes the awful timing of her question – motives being the topic, so she throws a hand up to interject. "Not that I suspect you of anything, Will. I don't."

"*They* will. I figured I'd disappear for a minute, give them a chance to bring some other suspects into the foal because as soon as they identify a convicted felon associated with a case, they get tunnel vision. They'll spend weeks trying to make it look like me, before giving up and entertaining other suspects."

"But doesn't disappearing make you look guilty?"

"I can't have my picture on the news not even as a suspect. They'll put my past out there for everyone to see. I own a business; my livelihood's on the line."

"I understand now. That makes sense."

"Will?"

"Yes?"

Ameena's arms folds. "This is probably just me, being me, but I am afraid, Will. That man is still out there. He pulled a gun on me. He looked me straight in my eyes like he knew me – or wanted to kill me. And that man is still out there."

"He doesn't have it in for you, I'm sure. It was probably

a random – wait…" He tries to look Ameena in her eyes, but she shies away. Will suggests, "Would it make you feel safer if I stayed? I'll take the couch."

Ameena falls into the man, hugging him tight, thanking him.

"Is that why we were out here talking all this time? Why not just ask?"

"Asking for help is the hardest thing to do for some people."

It's the spirit of pride and shame. Asking for help concedes failure. It explains why, on a hot Alabama day, Ameena was insisting on walking who-knows-how-many miles home, alongside the highway in a dress and high heels.

The convoy of motorcycles had roared by Ameena. She felt the road rumble underfoot, saw chrome streaks gleam. Will's head turned on a swivel. He held up a gloved fist, signaling the other bikers to turn around. They came roaring back, this time Will heading the pack, sitting deep in the machine's saddle, boot heels forward, head back; his image blurred from the heat rising off the road. Nine bikes lined up on the highway shoulder. Will was calling her, watching her walk proudly past him, ignoring his, "Ameena, Ameena? Hold up a sec. I can give you a lift." She ignored comments from the guys, Don't you hear the man talking to you? Is you deef?

Ameena answered them all. "I made it this far without help."

Will rolled slowly beside her. "Your car broke down?"

"I sold it."

"Sold it?! Look, don't make this harder than it needs to be. Hop on back," offered Will.

Ameena didn't break stride. "I'm wearing a dress, can't you see?" It was a royal blue maxi dress with asymmetric shoulders and a thigh split.

"In that case, I'll give you money for a cab, or Uber, then."

"No," she says, forcefully. "I don't want no money from no man!"

A double-negative from this proper speaking woman surprised Will. He let down the kickstand on his bike and trotted in front of her, livid. "I have had it with you!" He walked backwards at the same pace that she walked forward, but Will stopped and Ameena nearly bumped into his chest. She tried to go around him to one side and then the other, but he blocked her. "I don't need your permission to do God's work, you hear me," Will said, before going down on one knee and snatching the bottom of her dress. Ameena's hands rose as if she were being robbed and she stopped breathing, while Will did God's work between her legs. Will had hiked the bottom of her dress up and tied it around her thighs, more like shorts. He stood, wondering if he'd went too far.

Ameena began breathing again. She was panting and speechless, waxy with sweat. She would've obeyed any command just to avoid speaking. She got on the back of Will's bike. She put her arms around Will's body, securing her grip around his waist. She leaned forward and rested her face against his back, as if she were eavesdropping.

MONDAY

TRICK-BABY

NEW BIRTH members wake to a mass hangover. The memory pangs like a migraine, last night's dreams realer than the surreal yesterday. It is unclear yet how to own a memory that no one should own; a church-shooting. The word's two parts doesn't even mix, like oil and water. Words can't describe how that one day etches into your being – stalls you when you hear raised voices from afar or a loud bang from a dropped book – or how a red shirt in the distance becomes a red mask and suddenly you're seeing the red devil shooting the bishop point blank in the face, his wife's red upturned shoes peeking out from behind the pulpit, and deacon Smiley cupping an eye as red ribbons of blood stream through his fingers. Only years can reveal the extent of scars.

Preacher Shot is the headline on TV. Witnesses feel how horribly words fail, so they hush and weep as the news shows a nation in mourning. Mourning for them. With them. Strangers bring reefs and flowers and stuffed animals to the church's lime steps. Members phone other members, alerting them to turn on the TV, to see how their place of worship has become a national scene but hearing sniffles and sobs through the phone says everything: they, too, see.

Pundits make the obligatory calls for gun control while skirting the obvious – in this instance – that the criminals most likely obtained the guns illegally and regulations would only stifle those looking to obtain them the right way.

With Bishop Simon being the sole casualty, police suspect that the robbery disguised a hit. The spouse's cell phone records seem clean, but ongoing interviews of church members and leaders make a long, and still-growing, list of people who might've wanted the bishop dead. However, if by chance, the robbery was just a robbery, with no personal connection, it's no more than a man hunt for bandits who were smart enough to wear masks and cover their tattoos; police would have nothing more to go on than approximate weights and heights. Calls pour in about the vehicle; none checks out. At the top of investigators' concerns is the fact of Will, a convicted felon, leaving the scene.

They had come to his home the same evening of the shooting and even returned early morning, but he was not there on either occasion. In his role as the owner of Dantzler Heating and Air, he doesn't sit in a stationary office, he travels from site to site, so they can't catch up to him. The one thing police is clear about, is that Will is avoiding them.

The church's administrative offices close for the day, yet the campus is crowded. Inside leaders and elders hold an emergency meeting where they appoint Saunders as interim pastor. Reporters bunch in, as leaders exit, Saunders in pole position. He's New Birth's new leader.

The power seems to quench him; his posture shows it, as he approaches the press conference's microphones with his chest puffed out like a duck's breast, but then he's taken back by the flashing cameras and the volley of questions. In front of cameras, he mourns. Every well-meaning member who sees it, wants to believe this public wincing on the shoulder of a brother in Christ, over his private strut.

The country braces to hear from New Birth's new leader. They need to hear a wisdom that would release the pause button on their mornings, something that could open a space in their minds for which to file this tragedy. Javon Saunders's speech meanders for too long. The setup is forgotten by the time the tie-in arrives. He leaves them nothing more than sleepy ambivalence, much like his sermons.

Ameena receives a call from D'mitri Dalton, one of the producers of her upcoming play.

"You can probably guess what this call is about."

"My lines are seventy percent memorized," Ameena explains. "I just about got all my queues down."

"You might wanna hold off on that. We cannot stage *A Pimp In The Pulpit* in the city that just had a church shooting. To stage this play would be insensitive."

Ameena argues, "It'll blow over, D'mitri. Opening night is a whole three weeks from now."

"Huntsville was never a part of the original tour, to be honest. Before I contacted you. I got everyone except the lead actress to agree to amend their contracts because I knew your name alone would sell out the VBC all three nights."

"You can't cancel, now. What's Ticketmaster's fee for processing all those refunds? How much of a deposit are you forfeiting on Von Braun Civic Center?"

"Oh, believe me, it hurts."

"But it doesn't have to. If you knew Bishop Simon…"

"The Bishop who got shot…"

"The church is about to reach a settlement with a number of women he took advantage of. He had the church deny women help as a way to make them come to him personally where he then tried to exchange sex in return for money. If that isn't pulpit pimpin,' D'mitri, what is?"

"Wow… Sounds like Troy (the play's villain) in the flesh. Any outside babies?"

"I'd bet."

"Ok, I'll talk to Lynn –"

"– Lynn?"

"Pastor Evelyn Cummings-Stewart. She's the executive producer. The play's creator. It's from her life."

"No… How is this from anyone's life, like, how does a women's rights activist end up in a church that bars women from the pulpit, in the first place?"

"Is there a better place to worship if you're a woman hiding from the call to preach?"

"But the Ponzi scheme, the homicidal pastor – that all happened at one place and time?"

"I got a call coming in that I have to take. I'll run this by Lynn and get back to you, ok?"

Ameena could use the money. She needs the work; stars fall swiftly in the world of theatre. Plus, hospital bills are still rolling into collections, ruining her credit. She couldn't afford to take time off to deal with Rose's terminal diagnosis. Ameena couldn't afford to take time off to even process yesterday's shooting. On the news, an interviewee says it all felt like a dream. Ameena will never mistake that day for a dream. It materializes differently than dream or memory; it envelops her like the present and holds her hostage with painfully detailed images, like Simon's head whipping and spitting blood; the congregation's collective jolt at the shot, the panicked eyes, the stampede of shoes, a trampled toddler sitting upright on a gurney with blood dripping from his earlobe. While first responders picked Simon's lifeless body up from the altar, Ameena caught a glimpse of the exit wound, a golf-ball sized crater stuffed with ground beef. She cannot shake the image of the devil mask, down to the texture, squinting behind the double-barreled gun. There's a familiarity about that gunman that Ameena cannot shake; she fears he will come back for her. She wonders how she'll fall asleep at night without Will.

Will stands atop the Embassy Suites building, a mass renovation underway. He and the Wesley Construction's foreman game-plan for the arrival of the cranes. It's Will's first ever commercial contract. This week-long job will pay him three months' take. To ensure nothing goes awry, he would be on site, guiding his small crew until nightfall, ignoring his phone all the while. Police call from different numbers, but Will ignores any number he doesn't recognize.

Scoop, expecting Simon to be taken off the ventilator any hour now, calls a lawyer, pleading for an emergency consultation. Since Bishop Simon's estate is such an enormous pie needing to be legally split, Allen Brunn, attorney at law, clears a slot in his schedule in order to secure the case, knowing that with so much money on the table, his standard percentage fee would amount to a handsome sum.

Scoop's mother, Gene, comes in humbled like a homeless person taken in, grateful yet crowded by the furniture, caged by the indoors. She keeps ringing her hands as if her shame is a ball of clay that she's shaping between her palms. Gene turns to Scoop, her eyes wearing the pain it took just to face him. She sighs. She looks away, still unable to gauge how he might take the news. Gene is nervous, as if she's being prepped for surgery, her past, going under the knife.

Dictating the meeting is a typist who looks like an incorrectly matched sliding photo puzzle. Her tiny face above the desk mismatches the fatty legs below, her thick feet stuffed in strappy high heels.

Brunn thumbs a handheld recorder and signals the typist. He formally cites date, time and location, introduces himself, rollcalls the interviewee, Gene, and the challenger of Simon Bonneau's estate, Moses. Next, Brunn begins. "So, what was the nature of your relationship with Bishop Simon Bonneau around the time that your son, Moses, here, was conceived?"

This lawyer looks like no one Gene can confide in. He seems to enjoy his own speaking voice. His face, sagging with age, seems fixed in a judgment slanted against her. Gene delays by asking for clarity. "You say, the nature of my relationship with Bishop Simon?"

He clears his throat. "Around the time that Moses was conceived, of course."

Blinking and smiling through her confusion, Gene says, "But the bishop idn't even dead yet."

Irreverently, Scoop says, "He *will* be… As soon as his old lady pull the plug."

"The nature of me and Bishop's *relationship*… Why, to be honest, I don't understand why that's so important."

"A judge won't order a DNA test without good reason," says Brunn.

Gene pauses and then says, "Well, why would someone even *ask* for a test if they didn't have good reason?"

Scoop gasps, *Oh my God.*

The lawyer's hands gather in front of him. "Well, people do all kinds of things without good reason. If they're resentful, a challenge to the estate could be a vindictive poke at an already grieving family, so any judge would need some verifiable testimony before ordering a DNA test."

Gene considers the shameful things she'd have to reveal in the presence of her son and asks, "Can you ask Moses to leave?"

"Stop that, momma. Ain't nobody about to haul me outta here. Don't make me have to put my hands on these fine people, today, alright?" He lowers one fist; the other, he transforms into a pointing hand. "See, that's that same pride that has denied me my best life all these years. The least you can give me, now, is the truth."

Gene sniffles, her eyes turn wet with tears. "Forgive me, Mr. Brunn," she says to the lawyer, and then turns to her son. "Moses? I have a confession to make. Being that this is a sworn legal statement and I can get in trouble for lying… I need to tell you the truth that… for years, I've been lying to you, and to Mike."

Scoop freezes; his heart stops. He says, "I know you not fixin' to tell me that Simon ain't my daddy." Scoop is mortified, thinking that if his likeness to the bishop was pure coincidence, that he not only killed an innocent man, but surrendered his half of the money from the robbery because of an inheritance he would never see. "You hear me talkin' to you, ma?"

"Bishop *is* yo' daddy," she says, as she watches her son nearly collapse forward with relief. Gene continues, "I only lied about how that came to be." She turned to the lawyer. "For years, I made them believe that I was taken advantage of, but I wasn't." Tears stream down Gene's face. Moses leans over to console her. "Moses, here, was a good six-years-old when my husband Mike went behind my back and had him tested and learned that Scoop was not his son."

Scoop, holding his mother, looking at the lawyer, explains, "I remember going to that place. I was too young to realize it wasn't no regular doctor's appointment – nurse swabbing my mouth with a Q-tip. That day never, in any way, stood out in my mind, until one day… I was like twenty years old… high as a kite, and suddenly I remembered getting my mouth swabbed. I looked over at my homeboy Boon and was like yo, I think my pops got me tested a long time ago. I called pops right then and there, asking for the results, and that's when Mike told me he wasn't my biological father. I smoked so much that night, I damn near overdosed."

"Mike loves you Moses."

"I know, momma."

"The only reason he got you tested is because he just couldn't see himself in you, that's all. You was never the one on trial, Scoop; *I* was."

"I know, momma."

"Well," Gene sighs and dabs her eyes with tissue. "So, Moses was six years old when Mike learned that I had been lying to him. Mike went and emptied his chest of drawers and raked his closet clean. As Mike was dropping more and more of himself into that suitcase, I felt like I had to do something to make him stop. What'd I do? Lie some mo'." Gene sat up straight and took a deep breath. "That's when I told Mike that I was taken advantage of."

The lawyer cut in. "Was that the day that you told your husband, Mike, that it was indeed Bishop Simon Bonneau that sired Moses?"

Gene slaps her lap. "Don't say *sire*," she demands. "This ain't slavery."

"I was not aware of that connotation, honestly," the lawyer explains, apologetically. He finds his confusion mirrored in Scoop's face, as if neither he, a black person, was aware of that word's edge.

Gene bats away the awkwardness, granting pardon. "By the way, the answer is yes. After Mike found out that Moses wasn't his, I *did* tell him that Bishop Simon was the father."

"Again, my apologies for my wording, there," the lawyer says.

"You don't know what you don't know."

"Did you ever notify Bishop Simon? – The only reason I ask, is because if there is a last will and testament, and Simon knew about Moses, yet left him out of the will, he simply disinherited him. In that case, we wouldn't have a leg to stand on."

Gene's head had been shaking from the start of the lawyer's explanation. She says, "I never said a word to Simon. After our encounter, I never waitressed a table for him again, plus I found another job before my pregnancy was ever showing." Gene looks down at her lap and breaths deeply.

With this break in Gene's testimony, the lawyer offers guiding words. "Let's stay in this timeframe for a minute. So, you two met at a restaurant, not his church? How did you two come to be intimate?"

Gene realizes how far off they'd gotten, yet how therapeutic her trek through the whole truth had been to that point, so she replies, "I'm getting to that Mr. Brunn. I just want to tell it all, ok? For my Scoop –"

"– You mean, Mr. Moses?"

"We call him Scoop. Back of his head shape just like a scoop of ice cream." She smiles miserably. "Anyway, where was I? I made Mike think that I had met Bishop Simon by actually attending the church. Hell, I ain't never put hand on the doorknob until years later, but Mike had no way of knowing. Like I say, Mike was all the way in Decatur, Alabama at the time. I told him that I had counseling with the Bishop. I told him that that counseling was because of our broken marriage, so I made Mike feel guilty, thinking that, out of guilt, he might stop packing that suitcase and just stay. I told Mike I was exploited spiritually, but Mike took up his suitcase and left anyway." Gene squeezes Scoop's hand. "When this all came about, Bishop Simon's church was big by then. The man was rich, so Mike couldn't believe that I would turn down all that money by refusing to put the bishop on child support. Mike had a crazy suspicion about me and his cousin, so he believed that Moses's real father was his no-job-havin', baby-teeth cousin named Quincy –"

"– *Were* you and this Quincy intimate, six years prior to the DNA test – around the time Moses was concieved?"

"Do I look like the type to lay with somebody who got mo' gums than teeth? Lil bitty ole rat teeth, look like they been worn down from gnawin' on floorboards." The son, Scoop, doubles over laughing.

The lawyer says, "Yes or no, please – for the record."

"*No*, for the record, hell… Simon Bonneau is Moses's biological father."

"So far, you've told the story of how you misled Mike for the first six years, but we have yet to get around to *how* Moses came to be."

A solemn shade comes down over Gene – solemn, yet business like, how she proceeds right to the telling. "I had started working at this restaurant. It was a nice restaurant. White clothed tables. We wore white shirts buttoned up to the neck and long-legged black pants. Bishop Simon would come in every Thursday. He kept the same routine every week, says it helps to inspire his sermons. The day he sat in my section, he passed me a hundred-dollar bill on an eighteen-dollar tab and whispers: *for a tighter pair of pants.* Mike and me, at the time, were not together of course. And I needed money. Mike sent money, but nothing like when we're together, how Mike used to put his whole check in my hand. With his new girlfriend, he had a whole separate rent to pay, plus light bill, phone… I was hurting for money. So, with that eighty-dollar tip, I invested twenty-dollars in a tight pair of pants, and sure enough, every week, Simon kept the big tips coming." Gene squeezes Scoop's hand as she continues. "So, I kept chatting, smiling in his face and clearing my other tables in such a way that it gave him a view of my rear end, and that's how it was, until a couple weeks before Christmas. My only child at the time, Phoebe, was four. She wanted an Easy Bake Oven, a storybook record player, a pink Barbie corvette, among other things. She was heartbroken that her daddy was gone, so to soothe her broken heart, I was determined to get her everything on her list. My pay, along with the money Mike sent me, barely covered the bills, and I had no one else to turn to for money."

"So, you asked Bishop Simon for the money?"

"I didn't ask. I cried poor-mouth."

The lawyer's brow crinkled. "Poor-mouth?"

"That just means that I didn't ask directly, but I vented about my needs, in hopes that he would offer the money."

"Who introduced the idea of sex in exchange?"

"That day, when I cried poor-mouth, he pinned a hundred-dollar bill under his hand and says to me, 'If you want two more of those, you gotta meet me across the street to get it.' Directly across the street was a hotel."

"And then?"

Gene takes a deep, calming breath, readying herself to relive the nightmare.

The lawyer sees Gene's distress, so he holds one finger up at the typist and then asks Gene. "Did Simon rape you?"

Her lips fold in, a tear drains. "I'd have to say no, but… the way that man treated me, it felt like rape."

Simon had called to the restaurant for Gene, to inform her of the room number. She was disappointed that it was only on the third floor because she'd heard that only the top floors of hotels have the executive and presidential suites. After her shift, Gene walked across the street and went up to the hotel room, questioning every step, her hands and knees trembling. When she arrived, there was no wine chilling nor fireplace crackling, no trail of rose pedals leading to no bubbling jacuzzi tub – the level of class Gene expected from a man with such a refined taste in cuisine. What leapt to the eye was broken things, the patchwork of ceiling plaster covering a stain where a leak once was, the condensation around the window pane from a broken seal, the crooked grate on the climate control unit; the broken man; the broken woman, meeting in secret. Gene was twenty-six years old and was under the impression that she had seen so much in her life already that she could stomach even this. Simon was just a few years older but seemed decades more advanced in these dark dealings.

Simon raised his forearm, studying his gold watch. "I ain't got much time," he said.

Gene wasted no time approaching him; the quicker the start, the quicker the ordeal would be over with, she thought. There was no stirring of emotion that would make a kiss be anything more than a touch of lips; nevertheless, affection – be it genuine or blatant lie – seemed to be the proper start.

Simon, however, didn't want a proper start. He swerved away from the kiss, his head turning into a hand that combed back through his processed hair. His eyes sliced to the corner with a menacing stare. "I know you don't think I'm about to let your hoein' behind slobber on me with them big ole liver lips. Get undressed while I finish my drink."

Gene was shocked just to think, how, over a span of weeks, the man did nothing but build her up with praise, calling her intelligent, beautiful, graceful and kind-hearted – even complimenting the same lips he ridiculed – once he knew he'd had her in a compromising position, her baby-girl's Christmas in jeopardy, he was bold enough to show himself.

He held a glass of brown alcohol from the top, his ring finger tapping the rim of the glass. Once Gene was undressed, he studied her from head to toe for a full minute and then started barking out commands. "Now... Gone ahead and get on the bed. Boonk over. Now, back it up to the edge." He forced her head into the pillow. "Face down damnit. No peeking back, neither. Toot that thang up some mo'." He stood at the foot of the bed, dropped his pants to his ankles and did his business. It was the insults that made it feel like rape; this heavy, pulpit-preaching voice damning her with his thrusts – black, spook, dog, nigger, bitch! Oooh you pickaninny ghetto tramp! Awww you stankin' ass black dog!"

He finished with a violent seizure, eyes rolling up into his skull, mouth locked in a yawn. Gene balled up under the covers and lay there trembling and weeping.

Simon flung the money on top of her, saying, "I would've liked to let it go in ya face, but that puddin' felt so good, I just couldn't yank it outchya back." This, he says from the same mouth that would preach the gospels only a few days later. "Go ahead, cry," he added. "See if I feel sorry for ya. You got your money. Furthermore, your tears don't come from the same moral reservoir as those of good, clean girls. Your tears come from bestial instinct."

If Gene didn't have an appointment with her OBGYN as early as Monday, she might not have been able to deceive Mike. Less than a week after conception, Gene learned that she was pregnant. That same day, Gene drove all the way to Decatur and had sex with Mike in his car, in the parking lot outside his job; he worked nights. A week later, Gene called Mike to inform him that she was pregnant. Mike abruptly left his girlfriend in Decatur and moved back with Gene, his legal wife, with whom he already shared a daughter, on Christmas eve.

The lawyer asks, "It seems Simon was aggressive, abusive… Was there any point, in the heat of the act, that you told him to stop? Or was he hurting you, or…?"

"To answer your first question, there wasn't any point that Phoebe didn't need her Christmas, so there wasn't any point where I said stop. To answer your second question, there ain't no way in the world that man could hurt a woman with that lil' beanie weenie he got." Gene hears Scoop sniffle and realizes that he isn't snickering at her punchline; he's crying.

His head shakes miserably. "So, I'm a trick-baby? Huh, momma?" The lawyer waves for the typist to stop. Scoop gets out of his chair but doesn't gain any height; he's doubled over by the weight of this new burden. "Is that why I am the way I am? Is that why Phoebe's doing so good in life, momma? Because she was conceived out of love?"

As upset as Scoop was at his mother, he let her hold him and pet him. Strangely, Scoop is even *more* determined to give her the life she deserved.

TUESDAY

A MAN BETWEEN

WITH a vase of flowers in hand, Ameena roams the hallways of the hospital, questioning whether she should even be there, questioning the directions she received at the nurses' station. There are no stainless-steel double-doors where the nice young lady said it would be. Ameena is stopped at the intersection of four hallways, wearing a scowl when the sound of a man's voice spins her around completely.

"It's this way." It's Will in his biker outfit, a black leather vest over a white t-shirt and blue jeans.

"Will," Ameena says. By reflex, she hugs him with her free arm but then overthinks it. Does this hug draw up a social contract to embrace every time their paths cross?

Very gentlemanly, he takes the roses and offers his forearm.

Ameena hooks her arm in his and they and they take off. With panel lights passing overhead and walking at Will's quick pace, Ameena laments losing the option of sneaking up to the door and creeping away if the room is crowded. She could offer her sympathies in any setting, but Ameena's apology would have to take place in private. She and Bianca were friends once, but Ameena had used their friendship in order to get face to face with the bishop to ask for help for Rose's cancer. Since that day, Bianca hadn't spoken to Ameena. When Bianca sees Ameena, whether picking her out in the congregation, or passing by wordless in New Birth hallways, she doesn't see Ameena in the present, but sees her fixed in the betrayal and the guilt of that day.

Before Ameena could abort this visit, she finds herself staring at Bianca through the frame of the doorway, much like the day Bianca walked in on Ameena and her husband, the pair alone in bishop's study.

As they enter, Will announces that the roses are from Ameena, and he set the vase on the table. Ameena keeps close to him, feeling stage fright under the spotlight of Bianca's eyes, her husband between them like they day of their fall out, only the Bishop now lay in bandages, his chest rising and falling in sync with the hissing and hawing of the ventilator.

Bianca rises to greet them. She glitches, noticeably, at Ameena's grasp on Will's forearm, but she recovers quickly. "Ameeena," Bianca sings, as she shuffles over for a hug. The welcome is too lively and free, considering their history.

Initially, Ameena freezes, but then thaws under the warm, genuine feeling embrace. Ameena let herself trust it, let it stand for a nonverbal forgiveness, if Ameena would be so naïve to think surviving a church shooting together could heal their differences.

Bianca seems dressed for a ball, in a calf-high emerald green dress with a dramatic mermaid tail, six-inch heels, and pearls doubled around her neckline. She's always been a stickler for appearances; her eyes are fat from days of crying. When Bianca turns to next hug Will, she breaks down and cries against his chest. Will holds her until the wave of emotion recedes. He hands her a bandana from his

back pocket and she comes away sniffling and dabbing her
eyes while detailing her experience over the last couple of
days, of how little sleep she's had, of how horrible the hospital food has been. She says she only returned home
briefly to pack clothing. She speaks of how this sixty-
square-foot white cube has been her prison since Sunday.
She pulls her chair up beside the bishop's bed and looks at
him fondly. "He's lost a large part of the right hemisphere
of his cerebral cortex, is what they tell me, which is the
least necessary region of the brain, in regard to survival.
The trouble is, that the bullet scattered bone fragments from
his forehead into the other regions of his brain," she says,
sniffling. The bishop's sheets are pulled up to his neck and
his whole head is bandaged, except for the nose and mouth
which was capped with a breathing tube. Bianca adds, "I
have heard the distinct voice of God more, in the last few
days, than I've heard it in my entire life." Bianca places a
hand on the bishop's bandaged head. "God is telling me to
hold on. That Simon will live again, in due time."

Will says, "He *does* live again, through Tre."

"No, he doesn't," Bianca snaps. "No, he doesn't." She
then blinks away the cut from her eyes and set a gentle gaze
upon her bandaged husband. "Tre is Tre. And as far as
Bishop's other two children: Raquel is Raquel and Charles
is Charles. I'm talking about Simon *himself*. The hospital is
saying he's brain dead, that he probably can't breathe on
his own. But God! Simon Bonneau will get up out this bed
and walk out of here when God's ready. He gave me a
dream. A dream as real as us standing here talking right
now. In that dream, I was home, in my living room, languishing my husband's death, and suddenly there was a
knock at the door. Simon came through that door – not in a
wheelchair – but walking upright, unassisted, back straight
as an ironing board. And that man took me in his arms and
made love to me like he's never had before."

"T.M.I.," Will notifies, with a grimace.

"Oh, I'm sorry," Bianca sits, blushing. "I just get so carried away. This has been a lot on me. The staff refuses to even look me in my eyes because they want my husband in the cemetery just to free up another hospital bed. On top of that, I've been having to deal with Simon's daughter – that atheist – can't even put her differences aside, not even with her father on life support." Bianca's legs cross and her eyes fix in utter disgust.

"My Lord," Will bellows.

"If it wasn't for her brother, good ole Charles, I would rip the forked tongue right out of that serpent's head," says Bianca. "But that battle isn't mine. God will show them *all*."

Will says, "God is still in the miracle business that's for sure." Will drops a hand on Bianca's hand.

Bianca looks at Ameena with an air of one-uppance. "Ameena," Bianca says. "Do you mind leaving us, for a moment? It's something that can only be discussed among church leadership."

Bianca doesn't say a peep until the door shuts behind Ameena, until she and Will are alone. Bianca adds a third level to the stack of hands. "What I admire about you, Will, is how Simon is all but dead, and yet there's not a twinkle of ambition in your eyes."

Her piercing stare swaps the word ambition's new target from Simon's pulpit, and to Simon's wife. Avoiding her eyes, Will says, "Ambition gets in the way of God's will."

"People talking about Javon Saunders as a successor. He's married."

"That, he is." Will has to withhold his shock, for what Bianca implies, which seems to be a preference for a new bishop that's single, so she could – through marriage – extend her reign as New Birth's first lady. Bianca is, after all, the same woman who had rushed to the altar with Bishop

Simon before the dirt settled on the grave of his first wife.

"Javon isn't fit to be bishop," she says. "His wife isn't fit to be first lady – for obvious reasons. For starters, the first lady can't be no big ole wide-nosed bull."

"Bianca? I know you're grieving… you're upset… but Head Deaconess Saunders is an upright woman of God, and I won't entertain that kind of talk about her, or about anyone, for that matter."

"So, you'll cosign gluttony just to help her feel welcome? Even if it lowers the standard of what it means to be first lady? Don't you know that she used to work at a drug screening lab? Every young lady sitting in a New Birth pew deserves a First Lady to look up to, who models a sense of regal-ness and self-worth – who holds herself above stuffing her face with pork links and cupcakes; a self-worth that holds her above a career prospect of handling excrement for a living. If, by the slim chance that Simon does *not* recover, Will, I want *you*…" Bianca slips away in a daydream for a few seconds and then comes to. "… Sorry, I must be so fatigued, I lost my train of thought." She covers her mouth, realizing, at what point, she'd cut off her sentence. "Oh, that must've sounded *awful*."

Will smiles and nods coyly.

"I'm sorry baby, what I meant to say was that, in the event that it's *not* in God's will that Simon get up from this bed, that I want you – *to become* – New Birth's next head bishop. Jevon's got the interim, but you'll have the permanent position; I'm working on it now as we speak." Bianca moves closer, hip to hip, her hand caressing circles on Will's back as she asks, "What do you say to that?"

"Speechless." Will says, while wishing this woman's brain-dead husband could open his eyes and see who he'd chosen for a wife.

A nurse walks in, Ameena in-tow, but they seize at the sight of Bianca and Will standing so close, Bianca caressing Will's back.

Will welcomes the nurse, his rescue, but the nurse bows out, insisting that she'll return to change the bishop's bandages in a half hour, defining their slate to wrap up their intimate little vigil.

Ameena, considering what she'd walked in on, would've also announced that she was leaving, but Bianca speaks first. "Join us in prayer, Ameena – since you're here."

First lady offers the hand that would place Ameena opposite of Will, but Ameena sidesteps the offer and takes the other hand. "There we go," Ameena says, as she settles squarely and intently, between Will and Bianca, who had been inappropriately close when the room door was closed.

Heads bow. Will gives the prayer, but not without first lady adding background jubilee "All mighty, all-knowing God –

Hallowed be thy na-ame

We come to you as humble servants, as mere beggars, asking for guidance –

Askiiing

Asking for the full circumference of your loving arms, to hold us –

Hold us

To keep us –

Keep us Lord

As we await your divine mandate, while this manservant of yours lay wrapped in bandages, like your only begotten son did so long ago –

Oh laaawd

Oh, today we heed this shepherd who has held your staff of righteousness, has taken on every assignment, has exponentially expanded your kingdom and has stood unwavering even in the face of mortal danger – even offering his life upon the very steps of your altar –

Can we talk about it?

For your people's sake, God. We lift him up before you now. We come to you for healing, God.

Jehovah-Rapha!

Because we know that only you can do it. We can't go to family, nor friends; can't go to these whitecoat surgeons roaming these hallways, who curse your power with their grim prognosis. Make them eat their words God –

Touch and agree – huh!

Make witnesses out of these naysayers, God – make them yield and fall to their knees, God! These things, we ask of you, now –

In the might-taaay –

In the mighty name of Jesus, we pray. Amen."

"That was absolutely beautiful, Will." Bianca floats to him on the wings of heart-felt appreciation, nudging Ameena in the process. Ameena reverts, straight-necked, her flash anger rinsing away with the reminder that Bianca is grieving; all is forgiven. Bianca takes Will's hands by the fingertips and eases closer. Will backs away. "I've really gotta get going, Bianca. Yeah, I've got to go and uh… check on the er-um…" his excuse fades to mumbles. Will looks down to protect his eyes from Bianca's shine.

Bianca dips to hold eye contact. "You're too kind already for coming. Have a blessed day." Bianca comes in for the customary good-bye hug, something he can't deny a grieving woman. She pulls Will into her.

Ameena struggles to hide her disgust by not looking away from the display, Bianca's frontal hug, her veiny hands splayed on Will's back; her fingertips white from the force in which she traps him to her bosom. With even greater force, Ameena traps disgust behind the poise of a smile. Watching and not slapping the mess out of Bianca on pure instinct, is harder than standing in a swarm of mosquitoes and resist the reflex of swatting. Ameena almost does, when Bianca raises on tiptoe, slipping her chin over Will's shoulder, revealing the rivalry in her eyes, the gloating around her snout. Bianca's glare burns at Ameena while she says to Will. "Remember what we talked about, my brotha. I meant *every* word I said."

In that moment, a sociopath is revealed, as far as Ameena is concerned. The thing Bianca gleans, that Ameena never sees in any villainous character on stage, is the undercurrent of desperation – a desperation as dire as survival, as if Will is air to her – no matter how improbable to breath him, Bianca believes he is a finite resource that she must hoard for the dry season, and that he must be defended with teeth and nails, with the urgency of a mother to her litter.

Until that moment, Ameena couldn't fathom Bianca orchestrating her husband's murder. If the authorities could see how inappropriately Bianca embraces this associate pastor, the optics alone would steer the investigation to the spouse, instead of the convicted felon, Will, the uncomfortable one who squirms out the embrace, soiled by the sexual overtone of this church lady's hug taking place under the sound of her half-dead husband's hissing ventilator.

On the other hand, Ameena thinks, if authorities *could* see, maybe they'd suspect that what licenses Bianca to touch Will in that way, and then signal ownership to Ameena, is that Will, the felon, might be her partner in crime.

Will turns away from Bianca, his smile lost forever. "I'll wait outside if you two need to have a word with each other." Ameena sees the man turn away sullenly and wonders if it is mere performance. That question rings very small inside of Ameena – not that she'd seriously entertain it, but the question is there, nonetheless. Will is, after all, a convicted felon who is avoiding the police investigation.

The last thing Ameena wants is words with Bianca, so Ameena says, hurriedly, "Stay lifted up, Bianca." She nearly chases Will out of the room, but Bianca stops her in her tracks.

"Ameena?"

Ameena pauses with a hand on the door.

"Please…"

Ameena closes herself inside and studies Bianca who lowers into her seat and crosses her legs, her eyes losing its gladness. The blue contacts inside of woven eyelashes turns to outright menace.

"I will tell you this one time only," says Bianca, her lips scrunched over her words, giving muscle to her threat. "If you call yourself getting between me and a man again? I won't be so merciful *this* time. Do you understand me?"

Hair raises on the back of Ameena's neck. She is standing in the thing that nightmares are made of. "*This* time?" Her head swivels in truculent confusion. "Bianca, there was never a *first* time that I ever tried to get between you and *any* man. I know what you saw looked bad, and I don't know what Bishop Simon told you, but –"

"– You're just like the others!"

Ameena crumbles inside. "Excuse me?"

"I hope Simon gave you all the money you wanted, just to thicken its curse. That money will never bear fruit, you ole table-scrap dog!"

Ameena almost leaps. Her hands nearly rising to strangle, but out of grace she stops herself, the cancelled action redirecting her hands to her hips; that fighting rage still drumming inside of her. "Do not get it twisted, Bianca. The only reason I'm explaining myself to you right now, is because you're grieving, supposedly."

Bianca's eyes stretch as she matches Ameena's hands on hips. "Supposedly? *You* have got the gall to question *my* authenticity –"

"– Says the woman with fake blue contacts and bleach blonde hair."

Bianca draws back, her brows raised in superiority. "You *want* this hair and you *want* these eyes, but you can't have it because you know it would look ridiculous on your ole black-up self!"

"Black *up*…" Ameena laughs, but there is nothing chummy about this laughter; this laughter seems dangerous, where throat clicks are like bomb ticks.

"You *heard* me." Bianca touches the back of her hand to her forehead in exasperation. "I swear, that adjective beautiful gets thrown around much too loosely these days – as if it's every woman's birthright to wear that label. I look at you and I see the folly in that. Got some ole dingy looking, nappy-headed hoe like you, thinking there's a chance in hell somebody's gonna pick you over me? C'mon, now."

Ameena's hands go up in surrender. "If it's Will… you can have him, Bianca. But if you keep running that mouth, you and your husband are about to have matching hospital beds."

"*Try* it – you bad." Bianca takes a fighting stance. "I will lodge this thousand-dollar shoe so far up your behind, it'll give you self-worth!"

Back from the water fountain, Will enters and asks, "Everything alright?"

Bianca warns, "Will? You better get your lil ugly, scallywag friend."

Ameena, drenched in awful calm, says, "*Ugly*?" With a toss of her curly, natural hair, Ameena shoots back, "Well, ya *husband* thinks I'm gorgeous!"

Bianca begins removing her earrings. "*That* did it! Damnit, that did it!" She hops on each leg to remove her shoes while calling Ameena everything but a child of God. Ameena backs out of the room she points into. "Will, you better get her. She's crazy!"

Instead, Will corrals Ameena, using a half-hug to guide her down the hallway to safety, when a high-heeled shoe sails past their heads and tumbles down the hallway. Bianca doesn't lob the other shoe but stands in the doorway lobbing insults.

Ameena runs; she swipes the shoe off the floor and points with it. "If you want this shoe back, you have to come see me to get it – but best believe, it comes with a two-piece and black-eye-peas!"

"You ain't scaring nobody, Ameena. I will bring it to your doorstep – as soon as I find out which animal shelter they're holding you in." Bianca says, and slams the door shut.

Ameena storms down the hall en route to the elevator.

Will follows her, demanding, "Give me the shoe." Ameena walks even faster, the click of her high heels quickening with her pace. Will says, "Gimme the shoe, Ameena. This is silly."

"If Bianca wants her shoe, she has to come and get it."

"C'mon, Ameena. The woman's husband is on his death bed, she doesn't know what she's doing."

"You act like you care about this shoe more than you care about me."

Will is still hot on her heels. "Unbelievable," he sighs. "And y'all call yourselves women of God?"

For once, Ameena stops. She abouts face, her beauty vexed with rage, her eyes squinty and red, her ear turned to the insult. "*What* did you just say to me?"

"C'mon, Ameena. Can we not make *another* scene?"

Ameena's finger thrust like a joust. "I'll make a scene if I want to. You don't tell me what to do. And you don't get to hurt me and then tell me how to hurt!" Tears shimmer in her eyes. Ameena turns and walks just to hide her face.

Will scrambles behind her. "Hurt you? I would never knowingly hurt you, Ameena, I just thought that –"

Again, Ameena pivots, her fists down by her sides. "After saying what you just said, the fact that you're not apologizing right now, tells me *everything* I need to know about you. I will hurt myself just to *cut* you out of my heart." She even pulls an imaginary knife from her breast before walking off.

Will slows down to wrap his head around Ameena's words, what it reveals. If she can cut him out of her heart, it means he's is in her heart. So, every recollection of eye contact lingering, or a touch of hands prolonging, rushes back to him in the wisdom of hindsight. There is nothing Will wants more, this side of paradise. He shakes out of the trance. Ameena is getting away. He runs her down, his boots skidding to a stop. From afar, they resemble an eighties' music video, Ameena ignoring him while walking with a leggy stride; Will, the bad boy in a leather bikers' vest, walking backward in pace, as if pleading his heart to her in song, only his collars are not spiked up by his ears. But this is no whimsical song; the pair tread neck deep in emotions that could drown their relationship before it ever begins. "Ameena, I didn't know you felt that way. I… I feel that way too – not the part about the cutting you out, or nothing, but you are in my heart too, baby; you *way* up in there, like…" Ameena turns a corner. Will high-steps after her and hurries ahead of her, explaining, "I'm sorry, Ameena. I let myself feel ashamed of your actions, rather than feeling compassion for your hurt." Will drops down on one knee, his arms out in surrender.

Ameena stops and floats a palm. "Get up." She put her hands on her hips, scolding. "I said stop it, Will."

"Not until you forgive me. I don't wanna be no stalker, Ameena, but until you forgive me, you will see me every time you leave your house. I'll be popping up out of garbage cans, jumping out from behind trees."

She sidesteps him and keeps walking. "You're not funny," Ameena says as she bites her bottom lip and tosses her head aside to hide her dimpled smile – not that laughter means forgiveness. There're questions, still – questions she'll reserve for the opportune moment. She hit the elevator's wall button and waits.

Will waits beside her. "So, you're not speaking to me now?"

The elevator dings and the doors part. Will and Ameena play casual while people exit, and then they end up on the elevator alone, feeling the gravity tickle from the plummeting box when Will says, "So I guess we're right back to where we were before Sunday."

"Guess so."

Will tries humor. "You should be thanking me for not letting Bianca dust you off back there."

Ameena leans away, confused, examining him like a post-modern trash sculpture. The elevator open like curtains. As Ameena walks out, she thrust Bianca's shoe into Will's gut like a football. "You wanted this?"

He runs down a custodian wheeling a large garbage can and drops the thousand-dollar shoe inside. The custodian looks at the shoe, looks at Will and then shakes his head as if he doesn't even want to know. Will doesn't even have time to explain; he must catch up to Ameena. A man his size running after a woman who doesn't want to be bothered might rouse public concern, so Will walks briskly down the hallway toward the sunlit exit, like following Ameena into the afterlife.

Outside, the hot white sun glares off of every windshield in the parking lot. Will starts trotting after Ameena, but quickly feels stupid for it. "Don't walk away from me," he calls. "The way my pride is set up, I swear to you, Ameena, this would be our last chance."

Ameena turns in outrage. "Last chance? To be with you? Opportunity of a lifetime," Ameena says, sarcastically. Will keeps walking, steadily gaining. "Damn right, opportunity of a lifetime. You stopped, didn't you?"

"Just to tell you to go to hell!"

"You're mad at Bianca – not me."

"Oh?" Ameena twists; her hands gather in front of her. "Do you wanna know what Bianca said to me? She looked me right in the face and warned me – threatened me, not to get between you two."

Will's head lops forward. "*Who* two?"

Ameena's holds up pinched fingers, as if furious over two imaginary cookies. "As if *you two* weren't all over each other."

"*She* was all over me… I was trying to wiggle out of it."

"Wiggle out of it? You were basking in it."

"Look… When Bianca fainted in that church, she got up a different person. Something broke. You say she worships Simon like God, well, she just lost God. Just think: who would *you* be without your God?"

The thought staggers Ameena, not for what it makes her envision, but because of what it makes her remember. She knows who she is without God: a whore. In a more crowded city where neighbors avoid eye contact and where your name is not propelled around town by gossiping lips – in the reprieve from judgment that is Manhattan – Ameena was able to convince herself, without challenge, that her lifestyle was classy, vogue. Being *unapologetically free*, is what she called it. Her *craft* was her god, so if her sacred body was an offering that could make her ascend into the upper levels of theatre, she did it. She'd shamelessly leveraged a starring role, or two, between the sheets, including the role that won her the Tony award. She enjoyed excess – the finest of wines, the most luxurious of day spas, the classiest of restaurants, so surely she enjoyed the most exquisite men. In her multi-city tours with play companies, she picked men like produce and then blocked their numbers after leaving the city, and whenever she returned to Manhattan, there was always a waiting man under a year's-long impression that Ameena belonged to him only. Ameena knows who she is without God; she'd been without Him for several years, returning to Him only when she had a problem that neither her success nor a man could solve.

"Ameena?"

"Yes, um. I was just thinking," she frowns.

"Thinking of an excuse for why you shouldn't be loved?"

"I don't know why I said what I said, I…" She seems disoriented, woozy; only the right words could get her feet back under her. She looks up, plainly. "You're too good for me, Will."

Will claps once. "Sounds like a win-win to me – if you getting a man that you think is too good for you, and I'm getting a woman that I think is too good for me. We couldn't ask for a better deal, right?" Wrong. Ameena looks at him like he's stupid, which transfers into Will actually feeling stupid. Will, in his mind's eye, looks at himself and sees a big dope. His enthusiasm plummets. Aside from having a food tray slid to him through a solitary confinement chute, this feels like the most self-deprecating moment since; his forehead slimy with sweat, the leather vest in the hot sun. After no response from Ameena, Will chuckles at himself. "You know what… Forget it. This is starting to feel like I'm begging or something…" His head shakes insistently, "I'm out. I'm done."

"Be that if it may, Will, you're missing the point. Do you see how I couldn't even fix my mouth to tell you how I felt about you until *after* you'd hurt me?" The word hurt comes out arid and afraid. "You do not know my past."

"So, you got a past. Well, wha'do ya know, I just so happen to have one too, so how many more rabbits you got in that hat?"

"I know you have a past. You're a convicted felon."

"You're just finding that out? Heck, I refer to it in my sermons."

"Well, I didn't hear one of those sermons until after we were…"

"Hold up." Will's hands flop to his sides. "Is that why you started treating me like crap?" Will poses the question just to let Ameena hear just how small she must be, if that were the case; he stares her down, expecting denial.

"It's not that I'm judgmental."
Her honesty wows him and then disgusts him. "Unbeliev-able."

"But to understand why, you'd also have to understand –" She sees the man emotionally hurling away from her. "No. Will, listen –"

"– You know what, Ameena?" His head leans, his pointed hand is rowing. "I wish you would've never told me that. That's the one thing ya don't do to me. You don't hold against me what God has already forgiven."

"But you don't understand –"

"– No. Let me finish. See, I stepped in front of a gun, on Sunday, yet I've got detectives blowing up *my* phone. They refuse to believe that I did anything good that day. They don't see the business owner or the associate pastor; they see felon. They don't know me. But you? After all the time we spent together – a good year – in fellowship, and all the hours we spent together talking under the stars after bible study?"

"I tried to make myself feel differently, Will."

"What if *I* chose to ignore your answers and entertain your question marks?" He pinches his chin. "I guess I would be asking you why, after you being alone with Simon, your money problem was solved. And now you're having catfights with his wife?"

Ameena is shocked by her own evidence. It takes her a second to respond. "Obviously *you* don't even believe what you're saying, or why are we even out here talking about a relationship?"

Will seems to have lost his breath. He's lost something his panting can't replenish. "Why? Because your *now* is bigger than your *then!*"

That line, he delivers better than an actor, but they're not on stage; they're standing on hot asphalt. The high sun isn't stage lights; the rows of sunbaked cars is no audience. Ameena is no heroine and Will, no romantic hero. He doesn't throb with carnal desire and his words are not arrows through the heart. He is gorgeous, in a blue-collar sort of way. He is a preacher of the gospel, a heating and air small business owner, and a felon, professing his love. Regardless of who he is and where they are, what should come next is so predictable that doing nothing becomes *not* doing that: Ameena should run to him, let him catch her in his arms and she should kiss him with one leg kicked back – no red velvet curtain clapping closed on a presumed happily ever after, just the remainder of their Alabama day and many more to follow.

Ameena can't run to him because there is something wrong with Will – something edgy, something eerie and imminent that locks Ameena where she stands. He's offering another line of dialogue – a risky adlib. "I don't judge *nobody*," Will says. "And I'll be damned if I'm gonna sit here and let you categorize me." Parting words. Will turns to go.

Ameena yells, "I never took any money from Simon! Rose's cancer became terminal. We stopped treatments. *That's* why I stopped needing money!"

Will looks back. "I'm sorry," he says. "I'm truly am." He gives a whiff of wanting to go to her, but his sorrow for the little girl's illness can't cover his present anger.

Still, Ameena can't move, even as Will walks away. The asphalt parking lot could come crumbling toward her, flaking down into an expanding bottomless chasm and she couldn't save her own life.

Even before Will had jumped in front of that gun, Ameena couldn't stop thinking about him. The day he tied her dress between her legs, when she saddled the roaring motorcycle and put an ear to his back, Ameena's mind and heart had been in negotiations. Long enough, she'd let fear and pride keep out love, a thing so vital to the joy she prays for. She and Will had been at each other's throats for so long, they were stuck in the habit. Ameena went out of her way just to get a reaction out of him, her meanness hiding her need to have his eyes upon her and to hear his voice, all the while, hoping one day things would turn around. Ameena is more than attracted to him; she admires him. He is intelligent, but not in a manner that is forceful or self-satisfying. He'd offer a word or suggestion so light and free in its wisdom that its value hits late, like a picked highway flower, like a comforting caress that begins turning the day around for the better.

They should be together already. Ameena blames herself. She had backed away because she felt sick about mirroring her mother's facts: criminal boyfriend, fatherless daughter. But facts did not creep into Ameena's bed when she was just twelve-year old. A *man* did that. A convicted felon did that. Ever since, Ameena has feared the criminal element, no matter the crime, because her mother's boyfriend wasn't a known pedophile, until it was too late. He was a drug dealer, user, and a stick-up man. Turns out, the man was worse than his convictions. His civil disconnect was more severe than anyone predicted, so Ameena stopped predicting; any felon is her rapist's kin, as far as she was concerned.

Will, however, is different; she had to admit. He has a wholesomeness about him that even Ameena's theatre friends, the culture wolves, would seek to seduce and corrupt. Even before Will jumped in front of the gun, and after Ameena learned that he was a felon, she still couldn't stop thinking about him. Will may have walked away, but Ameena doesn't sense that it's over. She only hopes the handsome associate pastor is still interested in her after she explains to him that Rose is not her sister, but her daughter.

RAQUEL

Raquel looks nothing like the logical math professor that goes calculatedly about her days; she is emotional. She comes tromping through the hospital entrance, steaming, as if anyone who stumbles in her path could get it. She'd had enough of her stepmother even before Bianca decided to keep Raquel's dead father above ground, on the basis of ignorant hope.

Even while deep in the well of anger, Professor Raquel is driven by an equation. There's no durable medical power of attorney. In its absence, spousal privilege lets Bianca make whatever decision suits *her*, but the caveat is that Bianca's privilege stands only if she is of sound mind and body, which she is not, gathers Raquel. Bianca has been off kilter since the church shooting. All Raquel has to do is prove it, and then the decision to pull the plug would fall to her, the oldest child.

Differences aside, this is Raquel's father. Although they'd hardly spoken in the last three years, and stopped speaking altogether this year after her father announced his support of their state's abortion ban, which mandates harsher prison sentences for aborting mothers than rapists. Still, Raquel knows that seeing her father in bandages would be difficult.

Raquel stands outside the door and takes a deep breath before going in. Bianca is alone. She backs away from the bishop's bedside to let Raquel have a moment with him. If

Raquel really has love for the man, aside from the preacher, this is her time to lay down her sword and weep. There're no words; only helpless sighs. Considering their history, even idle chit chat could trigger a spat.

Raquel set her hand on her father's chest and realizes it is just that: a hand on a chest. No telepathic channeling of love; the math doesn't account for such things. The ventilator is just air flushing through a corpse. "When will you let him go," Raquel asks.

Bianca says, "I am not holding him against his will, Raquel. We both know who the real hostage is."

Mechanically, Raquel rotates to Bianca and says, "Even now, you can't help yourself."

Bianca leans back and crosses her legs.

Raquel frowns. "What happened to your shoe?"

"How is that a matter of your concern?"

"You're sitting up here with one shoe like it's normal."

"My other shoe is precisely where I want it to be. You think you don't need God, but that I must have a second shoe?"

"I've done just fine without Santa Clause and the Tooth Fairy haven't I?" With that fired shot, Raquel expected Bianca to get out of her chair, yelling, but not this time. Bianca just sits with her arms folded, perhaps knowing how silly she would look to stand, tilted on one high heel shoe.

Bianca stares ahead, over her folded arms. "Do you know what I did for a living before I came to Huntsville? I was a middle school guidance counselor."

"All I remember is you driving all the way from South Carolina in a hatchback Honda Civic. You were moving in. I was moving out –"

"– to *college*, Raquel. Don't sit up here and pretend you were made to walk the plank –"

"– While the dirt had yet to settle on my mother's grave! Regardless, I needed to go. Had I stayed to watch a side-chick, in your pushup bras and pumps, play the role of my mother, I would've ended up slitting your throat or mine."

"I rebuke thee in the name of Jesus!" Bianca's hand waves across her body as if splashing her stepdaughter with a vial of holy water. "That mouth, so like a serpent's… Sometimes I look at you and just wait for you to get down on your belly and slither."

"You started this, Bianca. All I did was ask about your shoe and you got smart with me."

The room goes quiet without sanction or truce, although it's still heated, the stepmother and daughter smoldering like sauna stones. Raquel looks away from Bianca, from any attempt characterize their silence as regret. Raquel studies her bandaged father, the darkest and most self-conflicting distraction she'll ever use in this life.

Bianca swaps her crossed legs. She pulls a stick of gum out of her purse and offers a piece, scissored between her two fingers like a cigarette. Raquel ignores her. Bianca says, "Don't act like you don't see me. And don't act like what I'm offering is only a stick of gum." Bianca waits on Raquel to take the gum, watches her slowly peel the wrapping and then bend the stick against her tongue. When Bianca sees Raquel glancing for a way to dispose of the wrapper, Bianca offers a cupped hand. "Give it," Bianca says. She sighs again as she balls the wrapper between the pinch of her thumb and forefinger and stuffs it in her purse. "As I was saying… I was a middle school guidance counselor. Yes, I was… I loved it. But every day it came home with me. Some children carry more baggage than us adults. When they're children, they have no power whatsoever to change their situation. We try to teach them how to cope, instead of us going into their homes and shaking some sense into their parents. I kept a mini refrigerator in my office. Some children came to me for TV dinners to take home with them, otherwise they'd go to bed hungry. Children came to me when they were bullied: bullied for wearing glasses, or braces, for being smart, for not being smart – you name it. You'd think the ones being bullied were the worst off, but that's not the case." Bianca pauses, noting Raquel's indifference, but she's too far along the path of explanation to stop. Bianca sighs and thickens her voice. "Kids who were invisible – who would go a whole day without a hello – wished they had a bully, someone to at least acknowledge that they existed. Still, the invisible ones weren't the worst off. Believe it or not, the children who had it worst were the little perfect ones… secretly crushed under the weight of their parents' high standards, the pressure to uphold the family name – them? They're more likely to hurt themselves. They'd take the dissection scalpels from the science lab and make cuts on their bodies. Cutting, is what they call it. There was this one girl, I'll never forget her. She made a hundred little tiny cuts around her genitalia…" Bianca stops to look at Raquel.

Raquel is staring at the back of her hand, examining her cuticles. "I'll have to get my nails done before the funeral." Bianca looks on in disbelief. "Raquel!"

"What," Raquel replies, her eyes refocusing from the daydream she was lost in. "Were you saying something?" Bianca touches her forehead as if she's suffering an aneurism. "I was telling you a story, Raquel."

"A *story* that would inevitably conclude with you trying to tell me how I should live my life. I am a grown woman, Bianca. I am married, with two children. I figure things out just fine for myself."

Bianca flicks the back of her hand. "Live your life however your please."

"Thank you."

"But you'll never find peace as long as you're mad at God. God is in everything; He's too much to be mad at."

"I'm only angry around you. You don't know who I am

when you're not around."

"Oh, yes I do. It shows up in your family. I see how they buckle the moment you raise your voice, how you treat Vance like a third child and how he bears it as if it's gone on for so long, he's grown numb to it. Sad thing is, you're not angry at them, you're angry at God. Well, you might as well be mad at the air you breathe because God is in that too. He is in the ground you walk on. He's in the love you have for your children. In the morning He wakes you up –"

"– *And a partridge in a pear tree*," Raquel sings, in grandiose fashion, degrading Bianca's psalm-like upheaval down to the level of Christmas carol.

Finally, Bianca is up on her feet, teetering on a single shoe. "Do you *want* me to knock the hell outta you? Because if you keep it up, I'd be much obliged."

It's precisely what Raquel wants. She smirks. "You came out alright, after all, Bianca. You won't have to nurse an older man late in his years while you're still young. What are you, forty, only? Still young enough to find you a happily ever after. You don't have to keep my dad on a ventilator in some weak attempt to make everyone think you really loved him. You could prance around with a hot young thing on your arm tomorrow and it wouldn't change anyone's opinion of you."

"Keep talking." Bianca kicks the shoe off.

"You've thrown away thirty-thousand-dollars since Sunday. Insurance only covers the ventilator for the first twenty-four hours."

"I'm waiting on this man to get up. I don't care if it's a hundred days."

The math professor replies, "And that'll be 1.5 million –
"

"– Of *your* money, boo-boo."

"What are you talking about?"

"Do you think you're talking to a fool, Raquel? I know

what's in the will, down to the letter. There are no irrevocable trusts setup for you or your brother. Now for me, on the other hand, what's mine is protected with our arrangement of assets, and behind ironclad wording in the will. So, ten days, a hundred days, a hundred thousand, a million: the moment it stops costing you and starts costing me. *That's* the day I put him in the ground, if God doesn't get him up from here, first."

Raquel never believed in the construct of evil, but her mother-in-law, Bianca, makes her reconsider. "Seriously! Your husband's killer is still at large, and *all* you're worried about is keeping his dead body out of the ground, so you can use this ventilator as a financial weapon, to bleed-out his daughter's inheritance?"

"Don't get it twisted, Raquel, this is not about you – you thirty-year-old, shit-ass brat. This is about Simon rising up from this bed, in due time, but what *I'm* saying to you, is this," Bianca's lips peel back to bear her gritted teeth. "*I could care less about what the wait costs you.* I'll shuffle the deck on Charles's behalf, make sure he's taken care of, but you? Out here grandstanding against Christianity, but now you wanna pull up to the table for this same 'Christian blood money,' – as you refer to it in your atheist blogs," Bianca says.

"What does your god think of what you're doing to me and to my dad? Huh?"

Bianca slicks the blonde curtain of hair from over her eye and says, "If God had one lightning bolt, and His choice of either of us to smite, girl, I'd be talking to a pile of soot, right now."

"When's the last time God struck down *anybody?* There's seven billion people in the world, and you mean to tell me that God can't find nobody to smite? Serial killers and rapist, sex traffickers?" Raquel's hands fly up near her face and she turns them into fists. "You are numb to facts.

You embrace the religion that justified your ancestors' enslavement, and you don't find that stupid? The definition of brainwashed: to *make* someone adopt radically different beliefs by using systematic and often forcible pressure. So, is it really faith if it had to be burned into your flesh? They forced us into chains, but now you wear those chains like jewelry," Raquel says, while eyeing a metaphor in Bianca's pearl necklace.

Bianca's head rolls back wearily. "Oh, shut *up*! You *know* I can't stand that blasphemous rhetoric of yours – plus my nerves are bad and I haven't slept in days either."

"Too bad because I'm just getting started. You're squandering my inheritance based on my opposition to a religion that warns you *not* to seek vengeance on people who would rape our women and lynch our children? It tells you be last in this life to be first in the next. If *one* plantation owner who force-fed you this belief, actually believed it, he would've given up his slaves to become one. *This* life holds all the marbles. Dead is dead."

"You will not curse our ancestors. It's because of them that we are where we are today. Do you know how many of them died for your –"

"– Died? They were slain! And if we were not brainwashed to turn the other cheek, history would also talk about how many of *their* ancestors lost *their* lives to revenge –"

"– Oh, darling, history says precisely that! You never heard of The Civil War?"

"That's different."

"Different only because it proves you wrong. You wanna talk about lives lost? There where were mounds of *their* bodies – fields of them. Whole surnames snuffed out of the record books for eternity. God turned them against themselves, for our sake, while we barely lifted a bayonet. If that ain't God's doing, who's doing is it?!"

Raquel is stumped. She itches to speak but has nothing to offer.

It's Bianca's first time seeing her daughter in law speechless. "Deny God's money like you deny His very existence. Or, acknowledge Him. Stop being mad at God for whatever man has done to you."

"No." Raquel rears back, head shaking. "You don't know what you're talking about."

Bianca sees a break in Raquel's belief, a stymie of her atheist conviction, and with this Bianca sees a yawning window of opportunity for her daughter in law's salvation. "As I was saying, Raquel. I was a guidance counselor; I see the hurt child in you. Simon even told me that you were a depressed child, suicidal by high school. You're angry at God's people for treating your depression, not as an illness, but as a *you* problem. Fault them, not God. They watched you sink. God was showing you your rock bottom so that every other challenge in life would feel small, by comparison. You had a father who tried to raise you with scripture rather than compassion." Bianca points at her husbands bandaged body. "Fault him – not God."

Raquel backs away teary. "You only know what dad's told you. You don't know *my* side."

Rebuking God is your way of rebuking Simon. That anger served a purpose when you were young and gasping for air; that anger gave you vigor, it kept you alive back then. That anger exists now as nothing more than force of habit."

"You're wrong, Bianca. You're wrong." Raquel's throat bloats with a trapped cry.

"Lay down sword and shield, Raquel. Pray with me, and you will get your portion of Simon's inheritance."

Coming into the room to replace a catheter bag that couldn't wait, was a nurse. Raquel didn't see a nurse; had the witness she needed. "So, you're telling me that if I pray with you, you will pull the plug?”

"That's exactly what I'm saying." Bianca steps closer, her hands out to join in prayer.

"I'll lead," Raquel insists, as she takes Bianca's hands, and their heads bow. "Oh, God. Here we are, kneeling to the old slave-master still living in Bianca's colonized head –”

"– Silly heifer!" Bianca snatches her hands back, anger and dejection grooved into her face like worn leather. As coldly as a killer, Bianca warns. "You gon play around get yourself cut, playing with my God."

Raquel's hand fans at her chin, under her cartoonish fright. "Oh my… So violent over a myth. I better not talk about Sasquatch or the Lizard Man either, huh."

Bianca's rage inflates her like a cobra. "We'll see if you're still telling jokes while you're lying in your own blood. Keep it up!"

"*Ladies*," says the nurse, while fastening Simon's catheter.

Raquel gloats, laughing with all her teeth, expecting a slap, but Bianca only feinted one. So, Raquel cut deeper. "Your God is as fake as your bleached skin – out here lookin' like Michael Jackson in the face."

Bianca winds back with a, "You will *not* talk about my God in that manner." It was on the word *not*, that the white of Bianca's hand whipped against Raquel's cheek.

Raquel had braced for impact by shutting her eyes, but the slap lit the darkness behind her eyelids. Raquel takes a dramatic fall, stumbling all the way to the far wall, pulling, and knocking down everything that she could. While in the process of falling and then landing in a seated position, the momentum snaps her head back into the wall with a thud, and then Raquel continues the never-ending fall by withering over on her side like a dying flower.

Bianca floats a palm at the melodrama while telling the

nurse, "Would you look at this? I barely even touched her."

The nurse calls for security, to Bianca's disbelief. "You're buying this act, miss? She was falling before I even touched her."

Raquel comes to, rising to a sitting position, scanning, gathering what had been done to her, her attacker towering five feet away. Raquel screams and scoot backs into a corner where she cowers in fear. Even the nurse rolls her eyes while helping Raquel to her feet.

Other nurses come in, responding to the commotion. Next, security arrives. All the while, the yelling can't stop. In less than a minute after the arrival of security, there's a tussle, as Bianca, wouldn't go along willingly. They hoist her up clear off the floor, one guard per shoulder, her feet pedaling air as she tries to argues. "That woman… You don't know her! She's evil, I tell you! She confronted me! She goaded me…" her complaints fading away as they tote her downstairs to holding in an empty conference room until Huntsville deputies arrive to book her for assault.

Raquel's plan worked. She now has the leverage she needs to have her lawyer to request a court order to evaluate Bianca's mental fitness.

WEDNESDAY

PRISONS

SCOOP makes an anonymous call to the hospital every day to verify visiting hours for Bishop Simon, listening for the day the switchboard operator would confirm that there's no Simon Bonneau occupying a hospital room, meaning the plug would've been pulled. In the meantime, Scoop is trying to find a suit; he needs to look classy to present himself to the first lady.

Scoop sits in a chair pulled up to the window. He bites his nail, gazing, waiting. Highlighted in the vertical band of sunlight where the curtain split, is his utter disgust for the woman he addresses when he says, "So you mean to tell me, all that tax money done gone, Shay?"

Shay looks up, ambushed by his judgement, her mouth corners rabid with ranch dressing. She first slurps a cherry soda then replies, "You *ought* to know. You helped me spend it. Maybe you should go ask Chandrika to give you money for a suit."

"That's what you don't want, Shay. So, why are you even suggesting it?" Scoop looks at Shay, like he's done with her. He eyes the belly stacked in her lap and how grotesquely she dips a fried drumstick in a bowl of ranch dressing. Scoop decides right then in that moment that he could no longer share a bed with her. "All that money gone… And what you got to show for it, Shay? You 'bout dumb as a ox, you know that?"

"Ya *momma* dumb as a ox," Shay volleys. "Ask *her* to get you a suit. Only a mother can believe that *your* sorry behind fixin' to work on somebody's job."

Scoop huffs, "*Job*… No. This is on a whole 'nother level. This about bidness – and in bidness, you can't show up in jeans and expect to be taken seriously. Here I am though, trying to do something for us and it don't even matter to you. See, in your mind, you're already retired, huh…" Counting off fingers, Scoop lists, "Ya got ya welfare, child support, food stamps, section eight, Lil Rick's crazy check…"

Shay set down the box and the drumstick and licks her fingers clean. "You ole jailbird. Who is you to try to put me down!"

"I ain't tryin' to put ya down, Shay. I'm tryin' to pick you up." He looks at her again and sees just how impossible it would be – figuratively and literally – to pick Shay up. "All I'm saying, is that if you rely on the government, yeah they'll feed ya, they'll even let you lay around on your ass all day, but the problem is, they make you do it in the slums. The slums ain't safe for your children. Isn't it just basic human dignity to want better than this – even if you have to work your ass off for it, rather than lie to yourself in order to feel better about yourself – like thinking you'll lose weight drinking a cup of vinegar a day while you continue eating this slop."

With sass, Shay dips a chicken thigh in ranch dressing and crunches into it. While chewing a mouthful, and smacking her gums, Shay manages to say, "You talkin' *real* big, right now – like you done got you somewhere else to lay your head." In mach surprise, Shay's eyes widen. "Oh, I know what it is: you *wanna* share bunkbeds with the winos down at the homeless shelter, must be. It's actually a step up from the prison I found you in."

"I'll put it like this: if what they tellin' you about me and Chandrika were true, I wouldn't be here. I'd be your neighbor right now, so keep threatening me like you're doing." Scoop hears the garbage truck and runs back to the window to see the garbage truck pulling off.

He springs for the door, shuffles down the stairs, wondering how he didn't hear the truck's arrival. He had tried to time the truck's stop to meet Old School out at the curb but got distracted arguing with Shay.

Scoop hits the bottom of the stairwell and shoots out of the mouth of the brown-bricked row houses, running full speed while balancing his ten-speed bicycle beside him. In stride, he leaps onto the bike, his head stooped forward, knees pumping until he catches up to the truck, with its hog-pen stench, and gassy exhaust.

Old School, who stands on the platform that extends from the bumper, shakes his head at the sight of Scoop, violating their agreement: no contact under any circumstances.

"Yo, Old School," Scoop calls. "Old School! C'mon, dawg. You ain't blind."

When Old School realizes that Scoop wouldn't go away, he answers, "Look here bruh. I don't know you and you don't know me. What's so hard to understand about that?"

"Ok then, stranger, lemme get a few hundred bucks. I need to buy a suit. You know I'm good for it."

Before the garbage truck fully stops, Old School hops off, hitting the ground running. He is the image of a man who is made for this, stocky, dense, bald, the gap between his teeth. He leans two cans back into his hands, and shuffles backwards, deftly, nimbly, like ballet feet inside of steel-toe boots. As he dumps them, one by one, into the large compactor at the truck's rear, Old School is saying, "You must not have turned on the news this mornin'. Turns out that old moonshine distillery back up in them woods was still active. Not only that, New York was still alive. He managed to crawl out of the trailer and onto the path before he died. A moonshiner came through the path yonder and found the body. An investigator called me this morning."

Scoop dies and awakens groggy. "Naw… What? But how though? How they know to call you?"

"From New York's phone records. Shortly, forensics will determine the time of death as Sunday, the same day of the robbery. That's when they'll start connecting everything."

"Damn," Scoop says while gazing at a bleak horizon. "This is all happening too soon, bro."

Old School looks around as if they're being watched. "Anybody who sees me and you talking is a witness, dig?"

"What if they find the car?"

"Nobody's gonna find that car. If anything, they lookin' for that car underwater, not underground."

Scoop swallows his stress in one dry gulp. He spots the garbage truck's driver, eyeing him in the side mirror, so Scoop cut the conversation short, giving the driver only his apparent ignorance to witness, as he says to Old School, "My bad, brotha. I mistook you for someone else."

Scoop yanks his ten-speed handlebars like horse reigns. He rides back in the direction from which he came. Scoop is afraid that police might be onto them. He truly fears returning to that massive, gray-bricked, barbed wire fortress that is the penitentiary.

He approaches the housing projects where he lived for one year of his childhood and where he now resides as an adult. A squad car rolls by slowly on his daily patrol. This massive cluster of brown-bricked buildings that Scoop must return to, is a lesser prison. Its gunmen aren't up in towers; they patrol by car, lurking like sharks. Barker project housing may not have razor wire fences, but it is surrounded by every social barrier imaginable. Pedaling slowly through the neighborhood, Scoop sees liquor stores, predatory lending establishments, over-policing, and their biggest barrier is that they're surrounded, on all sides, by a disproportionately underfunded education system.

As a child, Scoop didn't live at Barker for long. His mother comes from a good, educated family, but fell into this pit due to a string of misfortune. Gene then worked two jobs and did hair in her kitchen in order to dig her family out of it. Scoop, like his mother, could never be satisfied living in the projects. He is depressed by the fact that he, as an adult, not only lives there, but is pedaling his bicycle homeward to a woman of generational poverty, who identifies with this place, and is resigned to a fate of living and dying here. Scoop needs a suit. He remembers a bridal store not far from there and pedals in that direction.

There's a young lady hunched over in a stool behind the register, who only glances up from her smartphone. There's a woman too. She embodies the young lady's future self, draped in measuring tape, a pencil behind her ear, an eager smile. Scoop can tell, just by looking, that she is a one woman show, working the whole shop by herself. She's pretty, hardworking, dedicated, an entrepreneur. This woman and her child is everything that Shay and her children will never be in this life. He sees the mother modeling, for her daughter, how she should treat – even patrons who come in looking like Scoop – with the respect of a dignitary. It's unfortunate, Scoop thinks, that he's about to undo the lesson by stealing from her.

He tries on a white tuxedo, shoes and all; they fit perfectly. He sends the shop owner, Jamila, to the back looking for top hats, but the moment Jamila disappears in the back, Scoop becomes a white streak, flying out of the store, and then flying down the street on his ten-speed, knees pumping as he pedals in an all-white tuxedo.

You can't sweet talk a sinner into the church. You can only help the already decided, take their first steps. Everyone has their own motivations; for Will, it was a woman. He'd met her on a Sunday in the restaurant where he worked. Dawn, with that perpetual smile, came in for after-church supper with friends. Will, who held down a second job as a fry cook, came all the way out front to greet Dawn and her party of four. Will went far outside of his role to seat them with menus and silverware, and even a little humor. Dawn pinched his arm and invited him to visit their church. Will's manager wouldn't give him the day off, so he lost the job just to see her again.

One year later, Will and his brother, Buddha, sat in his car together, both staring at the engagement ring sitting in its box.

"Dawn pregnant?"

Will's eyes rolled. "You act like that's the only reason people get married bro."

"What if she says no," asked Buddha.

Will showed his brother a pair of lazy eyes. "C'mon, bro. This Dawn we're talking about."

Buddha nodded. "True... True. And you want me to be your best man... Me and my face-tattoo all up in your wedding pictures, giving the toast and erthing..."

They both knew the motivation behind this honor. It's Will's way of setting an example for his younger brother, by inviting him into the center of the event so Buddha could experience, first-hand, the life that's waiting for him outside of the streets. Will worried about his younger brother, who was sitting on his second strike and flirting with the third. Alabama's Habitual Felony Offender Act is their tactfully named three-strikes law. "All I need from you, lil bro, is an answer."

Buddha said, "It's all that time you're spending with pops, huh... Y'all riding round in that work truck all day. He probably preaching to you the whole time."
"It's called an apprenticeship. I'm doing work. Pop is paying me. I'm learning the business."

"Me and you, we different."
Even though Will could already see the wheels turning slower in his brother's head, from getting high off of his own supply, Will counters, "Our only difference is that you got caught."

"That's what I'm sayin' big bro. I'm in the system; I can't get no HVAC license."

Will's head shook. "The streets'll tell you anything to keep you there. Nearly a third of all licensees have a record."

"Furthermore, I can't be around daddy like that. He hit momma."

Will wondered how many more excuses Buddha would try. "The man that pop is, now, ain't never hit nobody. Pop always loved us. Still does. The only thing he did wrong was stay. He raised you and me under a bad marriage."

Buddha huffed. "Marriage… You gon' be pops all over again. You know what they say: sins of the father…"

Will studied his younger brother from the corner of his eyes. "You know what man… Everything that comes out of your mouth sounds powerless, bro. I'm not afraid of becoming pops. I got out of the streets because I was afraid of becoming you."

They heard the chirps of a squad car. The flash of spinning blue lights lit Will's interior, lit their stunned faces like lightning flashes. The neighborhood's high crime rate alone justifies stop and frisk, which the police takes full advantage of. With a felon in the passenger seat, the brothers knew the officer would use that as leverage for a vehicle search. Will asked the question he should've asked before welcoming Buddha in his car. "You dirty, bro?"

Buddha's head refused to turn. "I ain't goin' back. I'm fixin' to run."

Will checked his rearview mirror. The cop was busy calling in the license plates. Will said, "If you run, he'll shoot you in the back. What you got?" Buddha's head dropped and shook. Will asked again. "I asked you a question, Buddha. What do you have?"

"A quarter-spoon and a Glock."

"Drop it under the seat," Will said.

"No. You fixin' to be engaged and everything. You got a future."

"Everyone's got a future, but if you don't stash that stuff under the seat your future is a life sentence. This'll be my first offense – as far as they know."

"It ain't right."

"We both know I've done my share."

Buddha's head lowered onto his fist and he cried.

Will cried too but told Buddha, "If it turns out, that this sacrifice is in vain, Buddha, and later on, you end up behind the wall anyway? You lose a brother. I mean it. I will never speak to you again, man."

Buddha leaned into his brother and thanked him and cried, and then he placed the crack and the gun under the seat, hoping that the officer approaching the car was one of the nice ones; he was not. Will became a felon because of his brother's gun and drugs.

The cancelled Wednesday bible was uncancelled per Jevon Saunders. Ameena arrives early. More than ever, she needs God's understanding because her own has never failed her so badly, with making sense of Rose's terminal diagnosis, the church shooting… But if she plans on sitting through Will's bible study class, she must first clear the air with him.

She cannot set foot on church grounds without feeling the ghost of that day. Sympathizers mill around the menagerie of symbolic gifts placed at the foot of the church. Ameena isn't so early that she has time to entertain them. If no one else, they'll recognize the only interviewee talking to the news reporter on the day of the shooting whose bottom banner had a name, instead of a general tag *church member*, or *eyewitness*. Actress Ameena Mimms, in order to avoid the crowd, takes the side entrance where, in the building's eastern shadow, she runs into Will, who she named, during her tearful interview, as the man who saved her life. The look Will gives Ameena, regrets it.

"We need to talk," she tells him, and hears how cliché it sounds, how bad a script this line must've come from, but it works. Together, they search for privacy.

Jevon Saunders had uncancelled Wednesday bible study for a reason: to have Willie Dantzler hold still for the cops. Jevon sits in his office chatting with an investigator who had brought along a few officers just in case Will puts up a fight. On the walk into the building, the bald, meaty officer had stopped by a wall picture of Will baptizing a child. The meaty officer, cracked his knuckles and said, "Tha's a big boy."

This bible study trap was not the police's idea; it's Jevon's. He reclines in his office chair, the spread fingertips of one hand pinned to the fingertips of the other. He tells the group of lawmen how the robbery had to have been orchestrated by Willie Dantzler. "If you think about it, that shooting could not have worked more in anyone's else's favor."

The lead investigator is a redhead with lipstick to match; her face baked with clinical doubt. "No one else, except *you*, right? Seems to me, the triggerman promoted you to head pastor, idn't it? You now have the power, the prestige

– the pay raise…"

Jevon coughs and straightens his tie, as if his throat fattened. "Who me?" He takes his feet down from the desk and sits up. "I'm just the interim pastor. Will is the hero," Jevon's smile spreads, begging to be believed. "He's who they want."

"What gives you that idea?"

Jevon Saunders makes Detective Zeigler regret asking, how he whines about the coming Sunday, a fifth Sunday where Will is scheduled to preach. Jevon wanted to preach, anticipating news cameras, a nationally televised service, perhaps, because of last Sunday's tragedy.
Jevon's first order, as interim pastor, was to change the preaching rotation. His order was overturned by church leaders in an anonymous vote, so New Birth's first church service following a national tragedy will have the new leader, Jevon Saunders, sitting on the sidelines. The nation, in Jevon's opinion, needs to hear from New Birth's outright leader – not whatever preacher that the clock hand stops on. Jevon is the only man, in his opinion, who can, from the pulpit, inspire a worship service that'll show the world what people of faith are made of. Only he can preach a sermon that shows would-be terrorists that there is nothing, in a house of God, that man and his guns can destroy. "What the world *doesn't* need to see," Jevon offers, "is some ex-con preacher, up at the pulpit making it all about himself."

Detective Zeigler combs a hand back through her hair and says, "Even if we do detain Will, this wouldn't hold him out of the pulpit for Sunday. He'll be out tonight, depending on how he answers our questions. Just because he's been ignoring our calls doesn't make him a suspect."

"Why are you *not* suspicious? He wouldn't have jumped in front of that gun, if the gunman wasn't working for him. Will was the safest man in the building. Think about it: he's over the prison ministry. He's in constant contact with criminals. He used them to orchestrate the whole thing."

The detective clicks her pen and sets to write. "Great. Now, if only I can have the names?"

Jevon can't see the detective's sarcasm until he runs into the wall she placed in front of him. "Names?"

"The names of the inmates you think Willie Dantzler may have used to coordinate the hit that made *you* pastor."

Jevon chuckles and gives a measured, "Wait a minute…"

Again, he reclines in his chair. "You know what? This ain't even about the pulpit; it's about a woman."

It's the first plausible thing Zeigler has heard from Jevon. Ninety percent of murder cases are about money or matters of the heart, or both. "Let's hear it," she says.

First, Jevon spits the name. "Ameena Mimms." Next, he offers background on the relationship between Will and Ameena, which sputtered and left Will desperate. Jevon describes how bad Will had it for this woman – how the moment Ameena walked into a room, Will would stop whatever he was doing. He tells the detective how the pair would stay late after bible study, talking well into the night, but then something went wrong. They stopped meeting after bible study. They stopped speaking. And then they were at each other's throats.

Jevon leans in wide-eyed and says, "They say Will was mad because Ameena and Bishop Simon started going together, mmhmm. And that's why the only two people the gunmen singled out was Ameena and Bishop: the woman that got away and the man that took her away, mmhmm. But see, Will had his goons pull the gun on Ameena only to make himself look like a hero. Word has it that, the two later spent the night together – then they later at the hospital holding hands, so I guess his plan worked."

Zeigler is highly intrigued, but still there are questions. "We've interviewed about seventy people so far. Why has none of this come up? Who else knows about the relationship between Bishop Simon Bonneau and Ameena Mimms?"

Jevon pauses, daringly, and then fires, "Bishop's wife." Jevon checks his watch. "It's time. Will should be setting up for bible study as we speak."

Ameena and Will are in the bible study class together, alone, arguing.

"Will, how am I judging you when I'm telling you that I want you in my life."

"It's not about what you want, it's about you feeling like you're reaching down for it."

"You're an associate pastor, Will. And I'm a never-married single mother. Now, who's more of a problem for who?"

Will's brow twines. "Is this some sort of hypothetical type…"

Ameena's eyes clench, the darkness, symbolic of how deep she must go to bring back this truth: "I was raped… When I was twelve… Rose… Is not my sister. The man who raped me was my mother's boyfriend, a felon, so forgive me, Will, for being taken aback when I learned that *you* were –" She couldn't finish. Her age is regressed by this confession; she is twelve again, with her head down, and hugging her elbows. It would take the touch of another to bring her back from that small dark place, but Will's embrace is like none Ameena has ever felt. He doesn't attempt to pull her out of what she's feeling. He helps her stay in that dark place yet feel safe there.

They would've stayed in that embrace forever, if not for the arrival of the police. Will looks up when he hears the voice of Jevon Saunders who points at Will and Ameena's embrace as if it proves his theory.

"See what I tell ya," Jevon says to the detective. Will spies the red head detective and the three uniformed officers. "What is this?"

"Willie Dantzler," Detective Zeigler calls.

"That's me." Will steps away from Ameena as the uniformed officers approach.

"This is not an arrest," says Zeigler. "You're being detained and taken in for questioning, since we had such a hard time getting a hold of ya."
Will eyeballs Jevon and asks, "No kiss, my brotha?"

Jevon frowns. "I ain't no Judas. And you sho' hell ain't no Jesus."

Will merely raises his hand to point at Jevon and say, "All snakes look alike to me," but nothing agitates the detaining officers more. The meaty officer chops Will's pointing hand, saying, *stop resisting*. Will pleads, "I'm not resisting, I was just –" a nightstick whacks the back of Will's knees and drops him. *Stop resisting*. A scuffle ensues. Ameena is screaming, witnesses pack the entrance. An officer jumps on Will's back and rides him down to the floor onto his belly. Will manages to look up at a screaming Ameena and asks, "Is this what you want? Huh? Are you sure this is what you want!"

Ameena screams at the officers, "Stop please! This isn't necessary!"

Even falling is resisting, to these officers. Will manages to put his hands out to be cuffed, "I'm giving you my hands, man!" *Stop resisting*. Will is clubbed across the back, ankles and arms.

Jevon laughs and mocks, "Stop resisting."

Church folk squeeze in through the entrance, aghast. A row of pupils' desks fall like dominoes in the tussle. The church crowd screams at the officers.

Zeigler joins the protest against her own officers, "Guys, c'mon! Get him up from there!"

There's a knee in Will's back and a club under his chin. He can't even wheeze. Ameena screams, "You're killing him! You're killing him!"

Saliva and blood seeps from Will's mouth from a bit tongue. When the officers begin to look like murderers in uniform, church members jump in to enforce a law higher than the one the detaining officers represent. The sheep flex their strength in numbers; they do not scatter, they come in tight and it's the wolves who brace and then scatter.

Will drops lifeless. The officers are forced back out of the room where members examine what has happened. Detective Zeigler and Ameena kneel next to Will's body, Zeigler pumping his chest. Ameena providing mouth to mouth and getting nothing back. There is so much crying and morning in the room, around Will lying on his back, mourners look around, seeing a funeral materializing around them.

At the timestamp of 6:01 p.m., the church shooting is linked indirectly to a second casualty. Jevon Saunders gets the call from a deacon who is at the hospital with the deceased. Jevon rushes there. Already word has spread how Jevon taunted Will while he was being strangled, so the family of the deceased does not want him. It is the head pastor's duty, however, to be present at the death of a church leader.

Jevon is approached by the lead surgeon, his head still capped in latex, the mask down around his neck like an outlaw's bandana. He gives Jevon a rundown of the insurmountable odds. The attempts to save the life, so expertly explained with pulmonary this, cardiac that, is nothing more than a jargoned description of an O.R.'s hail-Mary toss. After failed defibrillator jolts, the heart had finally died outside of the body, in the surgeon's hands.

Jevon, listening keenly for material to color the prayer he'll deliver, needs one last detail, "The exact time of death? So, I can know the moment God called her home."

The surgeon smooths a sheet of paper back over his clipboard like the hair of a woman he'll kiss. He answers, "We've got Mrs. Ida Bethune's death timestamped at exactly 6:01 p.m."

Will is at the police station, sitting at a chair without a table, reliving the moment where he came to, consciousness opening like a curtain. He had felt the weight of a woman resting on palms pressed into his sternum; it was the redhead detective, pumping life into him while whispering a prayer. Ameena was in his face, her mouth to mouth becoming lips to lips, Ameena's kiss reviving this comatosed prince out of a cursed sleep. Detective Zeigler and Ameena Mimms had revived Will with CPR, Will's face wet with Ameena's tears.

Members had run to get Brother J.C., an EMT, who found Will sitting up, sleep drunk. J.C. did a few field examinations and deemed Will ok. The same officers who nearly strangled him to death, hoisted Will up from the floor and took him down for questioning.

He now sits in the interrogation room, Detective Zeigler pacing, somewhat gracefully, a novice ballerina approaching a leaping split. Without looking, she asks, "Where'd you go off to, on Sunday, Willie Dantzler? There was a shooting. You don't just go home and fix yourself a sandwich, my friend."

Will sits confidently; his solitary chair, a driver's seat. "I didn't leave the scene. Remember, I had a gun to my head. I was so shaken up, it made me sick to my stomach. I was in the bathroom, hugging the toilet."

"For better than three friggin hours?" Zeigler turns stoic. Her brow bends between insolence and disbelief.

"Yes," Will's nod insists. "Don't believe me? Check surveillance. The security camera in the foyer of the administrative office will show me entering that bathroom and won't show me coming out of it for another – I'll say, three 'friggin' hours is about right."

"Question." Her face says her question will be a disingenuous one. "How many other bathrooms you pass, on your way to the one on other side of the building?"

"You asked if I left the scene. I was still at the church."

"You're so smart, we ought to keep you here the full seventy-two hours – give us enough time to learn to be so smart, just like you."

Will's face shapes a smile absent of humor. "That's exactly why I didn't ask for my attorney. I *want* you all to misbehave – add harassment to that police brutality case I'm 'bout to hit y'all with. Fifty witnesses saw me choked for giving them my hands to cuff. I had to be revived!" Will coughed, his throat still raw.

Zeigler's head pulls from one side to the next as she sighs. "I'm sorry about that; really I am. But I can't kiss you on the head and send you home, on account of this case needing to be solved – like yesterday." Zeigler licks her thumb as if to hand out papers, but it's photos, a small stack she holds like house cards. "The world outside Bama is wondering why, three bad guys rob a church and here it is, four days going on five, and still this country-bumpkin, bacco spittin' police department hadn't bagged at least *one* of the three." Ziegler pops a card off the stack, which she rotates in front of Will's face. "Or maybe it's only *two* suspects left to bring in."

The man in the picture is dead, gunshot twice in the chest. Will says, "I don't know who that is."

"You should," Zeigler says, as she straddles a backward chair in front of Will. "Think P.T. and Work Release facility on Wheeler street."

Coolly, Will says, "Why ask me questions if you assume everything I say is a lie."

Zeigler's eyes widen, appalled. "This man, and yourself

were at Wheeler as inmates in the same population. Key-shawn – New York, they call him – later returned to Wheeler where you now run your prison ministry, okay? So, do I assume everything you say is a lie? No. But every time you do lie to me, I'm gonna make sure that you, one: hear just how foolish you sound, and two, I want you to feel yourself sinking a little bit deeper in a hole with each lie. Now, Wheeler is a small facility. Look hard at this picture and be straight with me."

"I'm telling you; I don't know who that is."

Zeigler's leans and frowns; she's curious, but game. "Are you playing with words? Is that what you're doing? I didn't ask if you *knew who he was*," she finger-quotes. "What I'm asking is, have you seen this face before, ever in your bless-ed life?"

"I know the face, but that's all."

Zeigler rockets up from her chair. "Gaw-*lee!*" She paces away and circles back. Her face dips at Will as she poses fists on hips. "If it takes that much for you to get off of something that small, Willie Dantzler, we're in for a night, you and me. And you can bet I'm ready. I've got a crock pot meal waiting on the kids – got a bough at home who'll help 'em with their homework and see that they get to bed on time. You wanna be a wise guy? Let's do this." She straddles the backward chair again and tosses her head back to clear her red mane out of her face. She is gorgeously Al-abamian, slightly tanned with an honest brow, and heavy in the arms. "Honestly, Willie Dantzler, my nose tells me you had something to do with this. You were the only person in that building concerned about hiding from us – the only one marking your whereabouts on a surveillance camera."

Willie answers, "Maybe I was the only person in that building who finds himself surrounded by three or more squad cars for routine traffic stops because when they run my background, they see felon. Or maybe I'm the only one who, just last year, called the police on my neighbor for threatening me, and they wind up putting *me* in cuffs. Once they see felon next to your name, they take everything to the extreme, am I wrong? Didn't they choke me out today?"

Zeigler is still appraising Will's outburst as she responds, "So you're saying fear kept you from answering your phone?"

"Why would I have anything to do with a robbery? I own my own business. I *have* money."

"What if the robbery wasn't about money, but a disguise for a hit?" She sees Will's reaction and smiles at it. "Changes everything, dudn't it? You talk about money; it's never money. It's the things money begets. You should know that. You spent four years shooting the breeze with killers out on the rec yard –"

"– Doin' my younger brother's time –"

"– Do they say they kill for money? Or is it power, respect, revenge… On an even deeper level, Pastor Dantzler, underlying murder is always a festering cardinal sin, like pride, lust, envy. Can I get an amen?" Zeigler stops, suddenly, a hunter's calm before the trigger squeeze. "Must've killed you to find out about the affair between Ameena and Bishop Simon."

Will sucks air, trapping rage in his belly. "Ameena and the bishop? No. I don't know who would tell you such a thing. Ameena merely sought him out for help."

"You, of all people, Will, should know that the women who came to Simon for help, wound up in bed with him. You were trying to take him down because of it, weren't you?"

"I wasn't trying to take Simon down. I was trying to get justice for the women. If Simon got voted out as a result, it would've been consequential. And another thing: I suspect maybe he *tried* to take advantage of Ameena, but she didn't buckle. She would never do that."

"She's out of money. And her kid sister has cancer, Will." A joker's smile sears across Zeigler's face.

"Rose isn't her sister," says Will. "She's her daughter – I just learned."

"Even worse." Zeigler squares her shoulders, flexing some force rearing up inside of her. "Don't *ever* think you know what a mother won't do for her child. On the way here, I made a phone call to the first lady, who told me she had walked in on Bishop and Ameena. Right. Under. Her. Own. Roof." Her finger jabs Will with each word. Zeigler examines Will's eyes and sees him concussed with the un-imaginable. Will remembers the day he found Ameena walking on the highway coming from the direction of Simon's home, and then at the hospital, he remembers Ameena flaunting to Bianca that her husband, the bishop, thought she was gorgeous. Zeigler adds, "Are you seeing it now? Love really *is* blind idn't it?"

Will cracks a smirk that discredits her in advance of his words. "You say you called Bianca… Isn't she in a mental institution?"

"If you were telling me she's blind, I'd see your point. Bianca *saw* them. Ameena was taken advantage of, but she's a celebrity, in the eyes of many; she can't come forward like the others." Zeigler's hands gather in front. "And you, dear Will… You were against Bishop on everything: the private jet, the visit to the White House –"

"– He went there to listen. I, myself, wouldn't have went, but I had no problem with him going."

She counts down three fingers. "Lust; you wanted Ameena. Envy: this abusive, low-life bishop took her from you. Revenge: you wanted her back even if it meant shooting bishop down like a dog. You even have one of the gunmen point their gun at Ameena just so you can jump in front of it – be her hero, so you can win her back."

Zeigler's pointing finger wipes across Will's forehead. She then rubs the fingertip against the pad of her thumb. "Associate Pastor Willie Dantzler? You are now sweating."

"Hot." Will pinches his shirt out from his body. "I applaud your riveting performance, Detective Zeigler, but *you* don't even believe what you're saying. If you did, I wouldn't be detained; I'd be under arrest. I think of all the disgruntled church members, the hurting families Simon refused to help, the leaders he's humiliated publicly, the political fanatics mad about the trip to D.C. and his support of the abortion bill, the fathers and the brothers of the women he abused, and I realize how the life Simon has led, has left you with too many suspects to sort through. I wish you luck. I really do." Will huffs and looks away.

Zeigler leans back and folds her arms, studying the piece of work sitting in front of her. "You're good. But that doesn't mean you're innocent."

"Since you're so busy throwing out theories, allow me," Says Will. "About a month ago, in the middle of a meeting, Simon suddenly got up out of his chair and said, in the words of Jesus, 'One of you will betray me.' Did anyone you interviewed tell you about that?"

"Nobody tried to put a theory to it like you're doing. It was assigned to Bishop Simon seeing his inevitable downfall and using it to sell himself as some sort of martyr."

"I couldn't have said it better," says Will. "Have you ever heard about the Gospel of Judas?"

"The bible I go by is called, *Thee* Holy Bible – now, which one *you* got? The most infamous snitch of all time has a gospel after his name? You have got to be kidding me."

"It was written about a hundred A.D., but the scroll was only discovered a few years ago. The gospel of Judas submits that when Jesus said, 'One of you will betray me,' that Jesus wasn't giving prophecy, He was giving a direct order.

Even the book of John says that after Judas takes the dipped bread from Jesus that 'Satan entered into him.' So, Judas wasn't evil; he was a vessel. Think about it, Jesus was never meant to grow old here. In fact, Jesus had nothing left on his agenda but to be crucified, so he assigned Judas the soul-wrenching task of turning him in."

"In your version, he still returns the silver and hangs himself, right?"

"Pretty much. The truth doesn't change."

"Back to Bishop Simon. Look, I'm no bible scholar, so please cut to the part where you tell me who was Simon's Judas."

"You saw the video, right? Isn't it strange how Bishop was the only person in the sanctuary unafraid? The only reason he confronted the gunman is because he was *already* certain of the outcome. He had the whole thing staged. He wanted to repair his image – make himself look like a hero, and maybe it would be enough to keep him at the helm of the church, but either something went wrong, or somebody had other plans."

"Here's the big ole hole in your theory, Will: what was the robber gonna do? Pretend to submit, let Bishop Simon embrace him? Hand over his gun? No amount of money would be worth the long prison sentence he'd get."

"But what if the gunman pretends to give his life to Christ, but then runs away, his escape shielded by the other two gunmen?"

"Pastor Willie Dantzler? You're working my nerves okay? I'm not havin' any more talk about Simon arranging his own death, alright? You're the one who has a link to one of the men we believe did this. Plus, we've got our eyes on another suspect that we know you had a close relationship with at one time." Zeigler presents another picture, hanging from the pinch of her thumb and forefinger.

The man is stocky, bald with a gapped tooth smile that

Will would recognize a mile away. "I forget his real name," Will says. "Everybody calls him Old School."

Will and Detective Zeigler talk at length about Old School, the owner of the last phone number New York called. The picture of the garbage man with the sketchy alibi was taken from a stakeout. In the picture, the garbage man's steel-toe boots seem to match one robber's steel-toe boots in the video, the one who pointed a gun at Ameena. The Old School Will remembers, from prison ministry Sunday worship, is actually a big fan of Ameena Mimms. When he learned that Ameena Mimms attends the same New Birth Baptist that brings its prison ministry to Wheeler, Old School began cornering members of the prison ministry, asking questions about Ameena, why she left New York City, asking if she was married or had a man and if all that hair was really hers. He was even curious about how she worships in church – if she sits and weeps or if she gets up and dances. "He found out that Ameena and me were kinda seeing each other and seemed really happy for me, but also happy for her because he thinks I'm such a good guy. I kinda hinted, one time, that Ameena was going through something – something she wouldn't disclose, but I told Old School that I thought that young Rose had cancer. Old School seemed really, really saddened by that. He would never pull a gun on Ameena."

Zeigler nods and reminds Will – warns him – that he has a link to two of the men they believe carried out the robbery, and that it wasn't looking good for Will. She says they went to Will's home on the night of the robbery and he was not at home. Zeigler now knows that Will spent the night with Ameena, perhaps the prize he won by stepping in front of the gun held by his coconspirator.

It doesn't help Will that when Detective Zeigler escorts him out front she sees Ameena waiting for him. Zeigler raises brows at their spirited hug. Ameena pulls back, saying, "Your car is still at the church. Figured you needed a ride."

There's so much to discuss, but the ride is a quiet one, the car dark, the dashboard interface lit. "You alright," Ameena asks.

Will looks down at his palms. "I've already done time for something I didn't do. I'm not about to let it happen again."

"They couldn't think you had something to do with it." His silence confirms her, but in that silence, Ameena re-hears what he'd said. "Wait a minute. What do you mean, again, for something you didn't do?'"

"My brother was sitting on his third strike. I claimed his gun and drugs so he wouldn't spend the rest of his life behind bars."

Ameena spends the remainder of the drive quietly lamenting the months she's lost with this awesome man, believing he's a felon, when it's only a technicality for sacrificing years of his life for his own brother. Ameena pulls up next to Will's car in New Birth's empty parking lot, under a starry night, and she remembers nights like this, standing outside of their parked cars, discussing scripture while taming her desire to lick his face.
Will gets out, their parting words, sadly inadequate considering the day they've had, considering the discussion left unfinished in the bible study classroom, and Ameena breathing life into his mouth, saving his life in return, their spirits now intertwined in ways she can't even imagine.
Will stops at his car door when he hears his name.

Ameena is hurrying around the front of her mother's car, her strides shortened by her high heels and tight dress. "Will," she says again. She slows with her approach. "You hardly speak the whole way here, and now you're gonna leave, just like that?" Her hands flare out at her sides, empty.

Will shrinks in shame. "It has nothing to do with how I feel about you. Look, Ameena, they're telling me I orchestrated the robbery to make it look like I saved your life, just to win you over. The more I'm with you, the more it proves them right. It kills me to have to pull back from you, after you done saved my life in return." He remembers her mouth to mouth resuscitation and wants another.

"But we haven't even *done* anything…" Ameena says but adds a word that shakes the world beneath them. "…yet." She sees how it changes him, sees him flex the tension out of his hands. Ameena takes a deep breath and wipes her palms down the front of her dress. Bravely, suggestively, she tells the pastor, "My mother's not expecting me back tonight."

With those words, Will notices she's wearing a different dress, not flowy like the earlier one, but this denim-like dress carves her out perfectly. Her makeup is refreshed, her lip gloss, wet. He glances in Ameena's car where the interior light shines because of her open drivers' side door. He spots an overnight bag in her back seat.

He reaches for her hand. His grasp snags two fingers, which he uses to pull her into his body. He pauses to look at her, taking her in; the moment amazes him. Experience has taught Will that beauty depreciates up close. Blemishes show, the impressive whole lost in its unimpressive parts, but face to face with this woman, Will doesn't see the porous surface, nor chipped edges. Up close while nosing around their inevitable kiss, he still sees the monument of a woman that he sees from afar. Ameena looks up at him and does not blink. Her eyelashes lower with his approach; his face eclipses the moon back over the horizon. The year-long tease of wanting him, waiting on him, despising him, being protected by him, and finally breathing life into him just hours ago, electrifies this kiss. Their lips join like the final puzzle piece that completes a picture of their forever.

They tease back, smiling sheepishly, for how foolish they've been to put this off for so long. They gaze, astounded, just seconds into their consummated relationship, wordlessly explaining how sought-after a treasure they've found – how this new belonging always should have been and should always remain. They kiss again, greedier this time; the reward of compound interest. They pretend not to know how this night would end, they pretend like they don't try to feel flesh through clothing, as if the kiss of lips doesn't create a kiss of bellies. Will pretends not to notice Ameena's cleavage, plump against his body. Ameena comes away pleased, her eyes thin with mischief. She touches her fingers to her lips as if she's just had too much chocolate sin cake; she's careful, though, not to be seductive. It would be unchristian-like to hint at what is sure to happen at some point this night. The pair would spend all night trying to make it look like an accident.

They must, first, have dinner. "On me," Ameena insists. Will tails her to an all-night diner decked with red booths, hanging lamps to match, and grey tiled floor. A jukebox plays an eclectic mix, from Otis Redding to Bruno Mars, and Ameena can't help feeling like she's playing the role of beauty lead in a box office romance that the beautiful women of her darker hue never get to play. She auditioned for *If Beale Street Could Talk*, and *Southside With You*, the only two real opportunities for a dark-skinned beauty lead in a major film, in her near twenty years of acting. Two. This new role, her real-life romance, is a closed audition; she will actually live what Hollywood won't let her pretend. Will is the tall, handsome underdog with a gritty past, and a pending investigation against him, her daughter has cancer – obstacles they'll surely overcome by the time the credits roll – is what Ameena would like to think.

They order whatever from the menu; eating is merely exercise. They match wits and they dream gaze, as if being together doesn't complicate both of their lives. They'll set reality aside for any number of tomorrows. For now, Will's mind is clear, his heart, a large football in his chest. Ameena looks at him and cannot ask for more. She has begun this relationship in full disclosure of the thing that has ended half of her past relationships: her childhood rape. In the past, whenever she felt a relationship getting serious, to be fair, she'd sit down with them, tell them that she has a daughter, a daughter down in Alabama who is just thirteen years younger; with this, she'd have to explain how that came to be, and she'd watch them take it unfazed, but only later to use that intel in an argument. Ameena learned to time the breakup – almost down to the precise week – when she'd hear her childhood rape come back cold in the mouth of a boyfriend using it to assess her worth. That's Ameena's marker to walk away. She knows, already, that Will is different. Will, the man who *don't judge nobody*, the man who so loathes judgment that Ameena found herself in the shoes of one of her old boyfriends, when Will walked away from her, in the hospital parking lot, refusing to be defined by his past. For the first time since Rose's terminal diagnosis, Ameena sees a future she's willing to walk into, because she won't have to walk alone.

The future is what it feels like when she walks into Will's home. She sees how badly she's underestimated him. The place feels like a palace, with its vaulted ceiling over the foyer, the winding staircase. They sit sideways on the sectional, facing each other, talking, each spontaneous kiss building to something they've seen coming a mile away. Will offers drinks, wine – their nudge and their scapegoat. By the second glass of sparkling Moscato, all the diner's jukebox songs come back to Ameena, playing in her grooving shoulders. She bites her bottom lip and pulls Will up from the couch to dance. There is no music, aside from the music in Ameena's head. The seduction in her eyes makes

Will put away his confusion and play along, dancing. The first song is a fast one. She's laughing. He laughs too. Their four shoes on the wood floor sound like a pony trot. And then there's a slow song, where she pulls into him, her head turned, her ear to Will's chest. Will guesses the jukebox tune, Anytime, Anyplace by Janet Jackson.

"What's taking you so long," Ameena asks. "Are you being the pastor Will? I want the biker Will. The Will that just does what must be done." Like the day he went down on his knees without her permission went between her legs to tie her dress up to her thighs like shorts.

She doesn't know how hard this is for the man, with his oath engraved on his heart. He apologizes to God in advance and he squeezes her buttocks, still swaying in the slow dance. His kiss travels this time, from lips to chin, to neck, to the bare shoulder he has exposed by pulling down one side of her dress. They are sure of it, now, while also sure that morning will make them wiser of it. Ameena helps him unfasten her dress and the material falls to her ankles. Will takes a half step back, leaving a hand on Ameena's belly to keep her where she stands, so he can take a good, long look at her. Ameena's lacy undergarments scream premeditation.

Ameena tries to step out of her fallen dress, but her shoe catches, her spiked heel slips and her ankle buckles. She tips forward. Will catches Ameena and her flailing arms. "I got you, baby," he laughs, thinking the mishap is done, but for Ameena, the ordeal has just begun.

She goes down to one knee, squealing and gripping her ankle. "This is *not* good," she says. She goes from kneeling to sitting. She's on the wood floor in lace undergarments and high heels, her legs stretched out, flinching every time Will touches her ankle.

He takes her in his arms, carries to the couch and examines the ankle again. "It can't be that bad, babe, it's not even swelling," he says, but one look in her eyes and he sees how their plans have changed.

After bathing and getting ready for bed, they still sleep in the same room, half sunken into Will's memory foam bed, like bronze, silk sheets over a large marshmallow. Ameena lays on her side, Will snug behind her, his arms tucked under her arm pits, their four hands interlocked over her chest. Ameena is surprised at how satisfied she feels; the lovemaking that never happened would've been only foreplay to this.

Will whispers, "I know how hard it is for you to ask for help. So, it makes me wonder if you ever asked God – I mean really pleaded to Him – on Rose's behalf." It's more suggestion than question.

Ameena doesn't answer, but she thinks about it while she lay awake for about an hour. She would have asked God right then, but she can't, not while lying in sin.

THURSDAY

Bianca's Release

Bianca would have been released a day earlier, if not for the delays. Raquel had her lawyer get an injunction approved through a magistrate court, ordering the psychiatric evaluation. They held her upstairs in the mental health population, pending successful evaluation, but the staff was backlogged. The other delay was Bianca's manic episode in the cafeteria, where she was held down and given a tranquilizing needle of benzodiazepine.

In the beginning, Bianca was doing fine. She did as the guards and staff instructed her, walking in faith, even while carrying an inmate's meal tray in that beige jumpsuit, her head down, denying the chance that eye contact be mistaken as an invitation to sup with her. Bianca only dared look up when there were no shoes pointed in her direction. She saw a woman sporting a jet-black mullet, her fingernails bitten down to the meat. Another, sitting upright in her chair as stiff as wax, but somehow the meal before her was being eaten; perhaps she'd only take a bite or chew when no one was looking.

Bianca's frustration of knowing she didn't belong – that she is not one of them, made Bianca unstable like them. Bianca invoked patience into her spirit by singing, mournfully:

Lay me at the throne.
Leave me there alone.
To gaze upon your glory.
And to sing to you this song.
Take me to the king –

Bianca cut the song and turned, feeling a presence. There was an older black woman with half her grey hair in plats, sitting next to Bianca but beyond the table's edge where there's no chair. The woman's face is dotted with raised moles, some as thick as chocolate chips. She was squatting, toad-like, licking, as if harpooning flies with her tongue. That was the trigger for Bianca's manic episode. She slammed both fists on the table and yelled, "Lady, if you don't get your big *jokey* behind away from me…!"

The woman went hopping away onto other business, but Bianca couldn't let it go. "Who do you think I am?!" This she said not to the woman, per se, but to everyone. "Got me locked up in here with these bunch of nuts!" Staff tried to deescalate while closing in, but Bianca couldn't feel their calming words, she only felt their closing in.

After the needle, she had slept fourteen long hours. She'd been sleep-deprived for days; battle fatigued, having a fight with Ameena and Raquel over her braindead husband's body, and another fight with the toad-woman. Bianca was spent. She would've slept more, but the therapist had finally worked her list down to Bianca's name. Sitting across from Bianca, the therapist eyes the report of the assault that landed Bianca in jail and then the report of her episode in the mess hall and predicts a sure fail of the evaluation.

Bianca's only worry, however, is passing too convincingly. She used to be a middle school guidance counselor; she has a college degree in psychology. Since becoming first lady, she let her license expire, but the evaluation basically hadn't changed in the twenty years before, so she doubted there were any significant changes in the ten years since. She can identify every bullet point of a textbook Multiphasic Personality Inventory test. Afterwards, they tell her what she already knows; she's passed the exam. They send her back to her room to wait for processing. She should be released by midday.

THE PAST ARRIVES

The ankle that steps out of the car door is bandaged. Ameena, standing gingerly with her borrowed crutch, still attempts to retrieve the Herby Curby from the street, but a streak of color zips by, saying "I got it."

"Rose?" Ameena's wrinkled brow gleams in the late morning sun. In the whole year that Ameena's been back from New York, she hadn't seen her daughter run once. Ameena tempers her optimism, as doctors advised. For Rose, it's a good day, not remission.

Charmaine staggers through the screen door, dying with laughter, a hand up asking the Lord for mercy.

"What's so funny?" Ameena can't shake her confusion. Rose running, Charmaine staggering to the porch in mirth – as if the whole world's gone mad on this beautiful morning, and Ameena didn't get the memo.

Charmaine spasms as if the new surge of laughter boots her in the back. By the time Ameena hobbles up the steps, Charmaine is weak, grieving with teary laughter, the porch rail the only thing holding her up. Finally, huffing and puffing to calm herself, she manages to say, "That ole Willie musta tore that thang out the *frame* last night! Sent yo sidity behind back on *crutches!*" She rears back in mirth all over again.

"No ma. Nothing happened. That was never *going* to happen."

Ameena's explanation only shifts Charmaine's laughter in higher gear. Her eyes stretch, her knees buckle. "You should've known from them big ole hands he got." She reaches out to brace against Ameena, and they both stumble and fall back seated in the porch chairs, Ameena nursing her ankle but laughing too, laughing at her mother's laughter.

Rose calls from across the yard. "Ma!" Neither Ameena nor Charmaine knows to whom she's referring. "Ma!" Rose is running again, wheeling the garbage can toward the porch – something inside she wants them to see. Ameena and Charmaine stand thinking something's wrong, and it is. Rose is terrified. She leans the can forward to show them. She spreads a trash bag inside to reveal that the can is full of crumpled money.

Each face checks left and right, seeing their own shock reflected in the face of two others. Charmaine screams, "Won't He do it," but then she hushes and spies for neighbors. The three women haul the can inside, stopping in the middle of the living room. Ameena clenches and relaxes, a tear spills and she wipes it with the palm of her hand. "What does this mean," she asks.

A nodding Charmaine has the answer. "It means that with this, we can afford to do something really nice for you, Rose."

Rose backs away, disowning it. "I've cost you guys enough already. Maybe mom can get her car back."

They check for Ameena's reaction and see her making a call. Charmaine resists the urge to swat the phone out of Ameena's hand. Charmaine asks, "Who are you calling?"

"Will?" He has answered.

"Ameena," Charmaine shouts in an effort to stop her. Ameena says to the phone. "I pray to God you had nothing to do with this."

"Ameena!" Charmaine wheels around aping language, arms waving like air traffic control.
Ameena went ahead anyway, telling Will. "Someone filled our Herby Curby with money. I think it's the stolen money from the church."

Charmaine turns to Rose and points at Rose's mother. "That big dumb momma of yours done told Will. Now we got ta kill 'em…" Charmaine rants on.

Ameena limps away and cups the ear not pressed to the phone, saying, "Garbageman? No one's usually home around the time the garbageman comes. Will, this doesn't make any sense!" Ameena, struggles to hear Will over Charmaine's ranting in the background. "Ma. Would you please?"

Charmaine returns, "This money is for Rose, no matter

what that man says. You might've been calling Will daddy all last night, but that don't make him family; this isn't his business."

Eerily, Ameena replies, "Come again?"

Charmaine's palm bangs the table. "*One* night and already you think you can call him in a crisis? You can't give Rose a father, Ameena; it's too late for that."

Ameena figures if Charmaine knew how much her words would hurt; she would have withheld them. Ameena is so upset, she can't even yell. "You go there? All because of some money in a trash can, ma?" Warm tears fill her eyes and spill over the wells. "First of all, ma, I've known Will over a year. Second, even if I wanted him as a father figure for Rose, it would be my choice. Remember it was *your* bad choices – harboring the fugitive boyfriend that crept into my room and took away my ability to choose this child or her father."

Charmaine surrenders with hands up, letting Ameena be as right as she wants to be.

Ameena remembers Will on the phone. She puts the phone back to her ear. She sighs to calm herself and erase the hurt from her voice. "Again, Will, what were you talking about? *Who* was always asking about me? Well… Does he have a name other than Old School?" Will's answer maims her. "No. Will. Trust me. You're wrong about this one. It's only been sixteen years, Will. He's got a lot more prison time left." Ameena turns to her mother with the same statement. "That monster's not getting out anytime soon, right ma? Ma! Is he out?"

Charmaine's face clenches. Her head-shaking no, is really an unspeakable yes.

Rose's fear gives her the chills; she rubs her arms. "Is *who* out?" She knows her father is a rapist, a predator, a monster. She's never seen even a photo of the man, but her fear of him is all-too familiar; her recurring nightmare now spat out onto the canvas of real life.

Ameena asks her mother the question she wants to ask society. "How is he out, ma? And you knew? You knew!"

Charmaine's mouth opens a full two beats before the first note leaves her. "I was afraid you'd go and take Rose up north. Her doctors are here."

"This money…" Ameena's swallow is so dry, it clicks. "It's from him." He whose name shall not be spoken. Ameena backs away. She backs away from the money that she so badly needs. She wants nothing to do with it – nothing to do with him. Even his memory, now, is overwhelming; it rapes her again. Ameena flails against it. Rose lunges into her and hugs her waist, putting herself between her mother and the ghost of her attacker, giving Ameena's arms something to embrace rather than fight. Ameena holds her daughter lovingly, and looks down at her, the spitting image of her rapist, yet somehow Ameena sees beauty and innocence. "God…" Ameena doesn't speak the name in vain; she speaks to Him with a salt tear melting at the corner of her mouth. "Look at this beautiful, innocent child. You have let cancer into her body. You let her suffer!" Ameena sobs over the child's shoulder, but then looks up, not in need but in contempt. "Why does it seem like you're blessing everyone but us! Spare Rose, God. Take me if you have to, but spare Rose," Ameena cries. Three generations of Mimms women embrace.

When Rose's grandmother, Charmaine, breaks away from the embrace to go peep at a window. Ameena remembers sixteen years ago, her own grandmother, Edith Mimms coming away from an embrace and parting the curtains with that same posture, as if looking out the window for an approaching storm. Ameena's history repeats with such accuracy, it mocks her. That man is out there now; he was out there then, a fugitive on the run, on the eve of their departure for Jamaica, New York, to go live with Aunt Debbie. Rose didn't yet have a name. She was just a solid line on a home pregnancy test; her family's worst nightmare come true. Ameena didn't know that Charmaine never reported the rape. She only reported the whereabouts of the fugitive wanted for not only violating parole for a previous crime, and for a new crime of robbery and conspiracy to commit murder. Back then, Charmaine did not want her young daughter, Ameena, to become a witness on the stand; everyone would know. The much-too-young mother and her little baby would be a public stain. So, Charmaine kept the child secret by moving to New York, and a year later moved back to Huntsville with only Rose, claiming the child as her own. Ameena stayed behind in New York where she was accepted into one of the country's best drama schools.

Hunting A Monster

Will is on the top of the Marriot's roof, the hot wind whipping up high. After ending the call with Ameena, he walks up to a man-sized duct and talks into it, so Buddha, his brother and crew chief, could hear him downstairs. He tells Buddha to meet him at the truck. In minutes, they spot each other across the lobby. Buddha's sunken back eyes seem ready to be upset. He thinks he's in trouble. "What is it *this* time, bro?"

Will asks, "Where're you parked at?"

On the way to the car, Buddha complains about having to stop work, and reminds Will of their time constraints. Will tells his younger brother, only, that he'll find out what the issue is once they get out to the truck. They're behind the building, near the dumpsters where the Dantzler Heating and Air work truck is parked. Buddha hops in the driver's seat and Will shot gun. Will says, "If I open this glove compartment, what would I find?"

Buddha sighs and bends forward, tapping his head on the rim of the steering wheel.

Will opens the glove compartment and pulls out a shiny nine-millimeter handgun. "In the company truck, Buddha? You're not supposed to be in possession of a firearm at all, bruh. You're a felon. And you still got two strikes."

Buddha tries, "It's every man's right to protect himself. The law can't give it or take it away, bruh."

Will nods. "Well *I'm* takin' it away – how 'bout that."

Buddha doesn't put up a fight; he simply shrugs and watches Will exit to supposedly get rid of the gun.
Will has other plans for the gun. He trots to his own car where he sits there and dials the secretary of the prison ministry to ask for the mailing address Old School provided upon his release.

Vicky asks, "Everything alright, pastor?"

"I think the brother might be in a time of crisis, right now, that's all." Will sucks at lying.

Old School's little shotgun home is across the street from a housing project. The yard is overgrown, the porch, leaning. The home could be mistaken for condemned. The paint is so chipped, the house seems to have broken out in boils. Will knocks and waits and knocks and listens. Will goes around back and looks into a window without blinds or curtains, just paned glass. He sees a pair of pants lying flat on the floor, a pair of boots on the counter, a cabinet ajar. Will calls Ameena again and tells her that Old School must've left in a hurry, either skipping town after putting the stolen money in their Herby Curby, or maybe he learned that the police is onto him. Next Will has to listen to Ameena's worry. She tells Will to stay out of harm's way. Ameena begs Will to come to her. She begs for his protection as a way to bring him to safety. While Ameena is warning him, over the phone, how police could swarm the house and mistake him for Old School. Will hears it happening as

Ameena narrates. He hears many cars pull up out front. Before he could decide where to stash the gun, officers were already surrounding the house, yelling with guns drawn. Will is well aware that he is a black man at the home of a fugitive. His hands are raised but still… This is the scene of his death, he thinks. He's cheated death twice in a week; it's ludicrous to expect a third time. "I am Pastor Willie Dantzler, of New Birth Baptist church," he yells.

Nerves bursts like camera flashes in his gut. He is a black man facing high-strung cops who are all shouting different commands, their varied faces all fired up with adrenaline. Will has a perfectly rectangle smart phone in one of his raised hands yet he's sure, he'll be a ghost in the hearings watching them testify that it looked just like a gun. He's afraid to even drop it, thinking he'll be Swiss cheese before it hits the ground. Will's hands are *up*-up, but he has a nose itch like he's never felt before in his life.

Ziegler shoots out from round the side of the house, her palms out, yelling, "Stand down! Lower your weapons!" Half the men listen. She approaches Will, the man they nearly choked to death last Wednesday. "Dantzler," she scolds. "Do you got eggs for brains? What do you think you're doing! *Put* your hands down, will ya? What are you doing here?"

"It was him. He was one of the robbers." Will is as spooked as a runaway slave.

"Ya think?" Ziegler's head kicks left. "Come walk with me." She ushers him out of the way, all along, fuming. "You've already been hero enough, ok? Comin' here, trying to shake down a felon. You: a felon yourself..." Her accent thickens the faster she talks and the harder she tromps through the yard. When they reach the safety of the sidewalk, Ziegler pivots in front of Will and pokes his chest with her fuchsia fingernail, her face just as red. "I'll tell ya what'll end up happening, you're gonna mess around and get yourself shot in the face." They're out to the safety of the sidewalk where there are so many police cruisers scattered about, it feels like a Madison County P.D. junk lot. They hear the battering ram take out the back door and then they hear the boots tromping inside like storm troopers.

Will explains, "I was only gonna talk to him. Tell him to turn himself in peacefully – to avoid something like this." *This* meaning drawn guns, the aggression.

"So, you came here unarmed?"

"Yes," Will says. His brother's nine-millimeter is tucked in his belt in the small of his back.

"I'm gonna ask you one more time. Are you sure you came unarmed to home of a man who not long ago shot another pastor in the daggum head?"

Will is ninety-nine-point-nine percent sure that the reason why Zeigler first asks if he's armed is because she intends to search him, but Will lies anyway. "I'm unarmed. I swear," he says, while in the back of his mind, he's channeling an internal prayer to God.

Ziegler squints and taps her foot, thinking, and then painfully decides to offer grace, in the form of her thumb hammering back over her shoulder. "You get your butt outta here, you hear me?"

Will dashes to his car. Nearly blocked in by the cluster of cruisers, he must perform a sixteen-point turn, jerking back and forth, sweating at the steering wheel as he cut left and right, pumping the gas and the brakes, before finally getting a clear shot out of the yard.

LEVI

Loneliness had made Levi Ginyard answer a call from a restricted number; it had happened to be the most important call of his life. The woman on the other end of the call had refused to give her name but answered the question that had been torturing Levi for over a decade – the child was never given up for adoption, nor aborted, but carried to term. The caller mistakenly hinted at their own location by saying, "The child and mother are living right here in Huntsville." The mystery woman had asked Levi to get pen and paper, to take down instructions.

It's those instructions now scrawled on the back of a store receipt, that sits on the Marriot hotel dresser. Levi stands in the bathroom mirror, giving his head a fresh shave. He knows that prison has changed him, and time has changed them both. He's much older than the child's mother, but he hopes that once she gets over the shock of seeing a man she had deemed a monster, that maybe now she could see the God in him, and maybe they could have a chance at love. Levi takes the receipt with the directions written on the back of it. The time has finally come. Levi drives his rented car to where the hand-written directions tell him, and he waits…

An hour goes by as he sits in the idling car, the A.C. blowing. He nods off sporadically, each time waking only minutes later, flustered, fearing he's missed his small window of opportunity, but each time he is relieved to find Bianca's car still parked next to his, in the hospital parking lot.

Levi is asleep again when Bianca arrives. Her stepson Charles has driven her there to retrieve her car. Tre sits in the back playing with a handheld game. Charles brings the car to a stop and idles. He says, "Why don't you come on over to my apartment, mom. You shouldn't be alone."

"Charles, I haven't slept in my own bed for almost a week."

"Well, I'll keep Tre for a few more days. You get you some rest."

Levi wakes when the Mercedes parked next to his rental chirps.

When he gets out, Bianca's hand is on her door, her back turned. Levi says, "Bianca? Now, I didn't want to surprise you like this, but I didn't have a choice."

The sound of that voice – that old Carolina Baptist pulpit voice – freezes her. She does an about-face to verify. Her spirit leaps out of her body. She looks to her stepson for help. "Charles?" Her voice is cracked and frightened.

Immediately, Charles sees the man's likeness to Tre, the kid brother born just six months after Bianca and his father's wedding, in which Charles stood as a teenage best man. Charles comes near his stepmother, guarding her, skeptical of the man in front of him; skeptical of the stepmother he protects.

Tre pulls the handle on the passenger door. Bianca calls him, "Tre, get here." He hurries around the front of the car to Bianca's side.

Levi studies him, a miniature self, scared behind his mother's skirt. "You've kept my son from me this long, Bianca. How much longer?"

"This man tried to murder my best friend, Nay," she whimpers to her boys.

Charles knows he's in over his head, facing a killer. He pulls out his phone.

Levi corrects her, "And you had an affair with your best friend's husband. The only reason you and me aren't together right now is because my plan failed." Levi drops a hand on his head and shakes. "I ain't no killer. I wasn't myself, then."

Charles can't look at his stepmother, nor the man who

makes Raquel right for hating Bianca and himself wrong for always omitting the 'step' in front of mom.

Bianca puts a hand on each of her boys. "Behold Satan. The truth is not in him. He is a serpent! He is a liar!"

Levi creeps forward. "I may be a liar but everything I just said is no lie. And that boy there is my son."

"Get back," Bianca stiff-arms an aerosol of pepper spray on her keychain. "Tre is not your son. He is the last-born son of Bishop Simon Lawrence Bonneau!"

"Girl, who you think you tellin'? I been lookin' in the face of Ginyard kin all my life. That boy there is family. Look at the thick skull, the strawberry nose. You wear glasses son?"

"Yes sir."

"Shut up, Tre!" Bianca holds out the pepper spray at arm's length threatening him, as she gets into her car and as Charles takes his younger brother to his car, and they drive off, leaving Levi there.

LEVI AND RAQUEL

Raquel is at a hotel bar with her legs crossed. She sips a flute of champagne, wearily, as if she's just lost a political race; now drinking champagne meant for victory, to sooth the agony of defeat. She's learned that her plan A failed; Bianca passed the mental health evaluation. Plan B failed too. Bianca hasn't pulled the plug herself to ensure that Simon dies oblivious to Tre's paternity.

There is no plan C. So, Raquel sips wine at a bar alone, sulking over her failed effort to thwart the evil Bianca – but then Raquel edits her thoughts because if there is such a thing as evil, it must have a champion, Satan, meaning good also has its champion – but she doesn't believe in God. Raquel believes in science and mathematics. She believes in the Theory of Relativity. But if Bianca can't be evil, being merely an indifferent equal of an opposite force is an upgrade indeed. But doesn't Relativity, too, have its champion? Raquel feels her thoughts turning into a whirlpool. She's had one too many glasses of champagne, Raquel thinks, as she sips again.

She tries to quit her thoughts but can't. Her whole life has been defined by what it refutes. What are the chances of her father miraculously recovering? The Theory of Probability actually accounts for such seemingly impossible things: if it *can* happen, it will – if given infinite variables and time. A monkey playing on a keyboard for eternity will eventually, and accidentally, type out the complete works of Shakespeare. Her father doesn't have infinite time. It would be a miracle for him to wake up. Again, Raquel edits out the word miracle, which implies the divine, when there is no such thing. The chance of her father recovering is a universal dice-roll. So, instead of outright denying the chance that her father could wake up, Raquel admits that it can happen, but figures the odds are so astronomical, it kills her hope and makes her feel depressed. Raquel sighs and admits that it aches to be inside of her head during crises. Her logic can't stop her from wanting a proper burial for her father, next to her mother, his first wife – his only wife, in Raquel's mind. Bianca still might pull the plug, Raquel hopes. Raquel sighs just thinking of all the ignorant Christians she'd have to entertain, with their prayers and scriptures throughout the wake, gatherings and the funeral. She shudders, downs her champagne glass and signals for another.

Raquel's nose, the very profile of her father's, lifts upward to the television where the news reports how the church money from the robbery was dumped in the trash can of Broadway actress Ameena Mimms who then turned the money in to police. They post a picture of the baldheaded fugitive at-large, his name befitting an aging boxer, Lonnie "Old School" Brown.

Another baldheaded man enters the bar. Levi has never seen Raquel's face, only heard her voice over the phone, so she helps him out with a wave. He's already told her over the phone how badly the visit went, however, it is no concern of Raquel's; she's already gotten what she needed of him. She tries to order him a beer. "Ginger Ale," he prefers. Levi hikes up his belt and sits at the stool next to Raquel. He says, morbidly, "I've spent over a couple years looking for Bianca. I can't tell you how much I appreciate the help."

Raquel bites down on her first words and chooses a milder response. "I was helping myself. The estate will now be split between two children and instead of three."

Levi studies the pop set down in front of him. "Well, thank you anyway."

"I thought Bianca would've come clean. There's no way she could deny that Tre is yours." Raquel feels a plan C developing. "That being said, if she doesn't take him off of the ventilator in a few days, I might need you again."

"As long as your needs are in line with my needs."

"I'm listening."

"I want a relationship with my son."

Raquel twitches to him, her eyes inquisitive. "How long before you go back to South Carolina?"

"Until I can at least get a sit down with Tre. Maybe a week."

"Good. That's enough time to get a court order for a DNA test. I have lawyers and they're good."

Levi's head twists to his right shoulder, his face embittered. "Why all the schemes, though? You ever try just talking to her?"

"The last time I tried that, security had to haul her off to jail for assaulting me."

"Sorry to hear."

"No love lost. We've always hated each other." With his advice killed and Raquel having nothing else really to say, both turn their drinks up. Levi, then squints from a hard swallow and says, "Why don't you just give me Bianca's address?"

"The address is unpublished, and with good reason. Do you know how many people would randomly show up at a pastor's home?"

"I ain't asking you to list the address. Just give it to *me*."

"I hate Bianca's guts, but not enough to give her address to someone like you," Raquel says. Levi leans in, crowding Raquel but before he could plead with her, Raquel kills it with the white of her hand. "Dude. You were already convicted for trying to kill the mother of your child. And you're asking me to give you the address of the mother of your *other* child?"

Levi tries, "But what if your child was –" he stops at the sight of Raquel's stare down. Levi huffs and says, "Never mind."

Raquel's hands join at the foot of her wine glass. She looks over and says, "Know why she's keeping him on that ventilator? On the one hand, she's using that ten thousand dollar a day weapon to drain my inheritance, and on the other, she believes God's about to stir the clouds with his finger and make Simon get up out of that hospital bed and walk. Heck, he can't even breathe – something we all can do in our sleep," she says with an open hand, the obvious sitting in her palm.

Levi, the former pastor, replies, "I've seen wilder miracles than that. You should be careful about doubting the Master."

Raquel rests her chin on her knuckles, eyeing the man like a sniper through the scope. "Are you really sitting here, talking about God? I talked to Pastor Lynn Stewart –"

"– Lynn!?"

"She says you beat your wife. She said you slammed your wife's face down into an open bible while you raped her from behind. I'm an atheist – for your information – and I'd never even *think* of doing things you actually carried out –"

"– Yet *you'll* be the one burning in hell, while I'll be forgiven," Levi exclaims, as he backs away from the bar.

"Good day, sir," Raquel says with reddened eyes. Levi rebukes her as he's walking away, but Raquel drowns him out with her facetious farewells. "Drive safe, rapist! Take care, wife-beater!" Stunned dining room guests lean and whisper.

The bartender considers cutting Raquel off. Wearing a puppet's smile, he inquires if she's staying at the hotel, which gives Raquel the idea. "Yes, actually." She books a room using her smartphone and then goes to the front desk to get the room key. She returns to the same barstool, now talking on the phone with her husband telling him how it's been such a long day, and although she knows it's only a forty-five minute drive home, it's not one she's up for, plus she's had one drink too many. While she's on the phone talking with her husband, she notices a woman sitting a few seats down from her. She keeps on talking with her husband, but her eyes stay on the woman.

The woman has a small fro, golden and wavy. She sports aggressive hoop earrings that Raquel would only dare to wear as an accessory to a costume. The woman has this executive presence, this self-assured maturity that Raquel would love to borrow for a day. The small tattoo on the back of her neck and the longer one on her muscular calf will say, to most, that this woman has a past. What it says to Raquel, the preacher's daughter, is that this woman has lived.

The woman asks the bartender to start a tab. When she hands over her card, the back of her arm ripples like a wrung towel. She has the body and grace of a retired ballerina. Just sitting there, simply waiting on a drink, the woman sizzles with anticipation.

Raquel hears her name and remembers her husband on the phone. "Yes dear. I'm sorry I just… Anyway, I'll call you back when I'm tucked in, ok love? I love you too. Bye-bye hon."

Raquel puts away her phone and says to the woman. "Excuse me? Don't take this the wrong way, but I think you are so beautiful."

The woman leans away, her chin tucked, brows up. "How many drinks have you had?"

Raquel laughs, her mirth overdone.

The woman swivels to the bartender but thumbs back at Raquel. "I'll have what she's having."

They're all smiles, their little community of three, but then the moment dies and they're all back to their individual worlds.

Raquel eyes the Chevy keyring. A tipsy Raquel thinks the coincidence of having the same cars is enough to carry a conversation. "Equinox?"

The woman winces at how wrong. "Camaro baby."

"No offense intended," Raquel smiles.

"None taken," replies the woman. "Tori." She offers a handshake which Raquel promptly accepts.

"Raquel. Charmed."

The two become fast friends, Raquel, the self-conscious math professor, and Tori, the divorced physical therapist-slash-personal trainer who has this certain sway about her as if sultry jazz is chiming through the speakers in her mind. She's driven down from Jackson, MS.

Raquel notices there's no wedding ring. "Never married?"

"I only wish I was never married," Tori kids. "Who were you talking to on the phone earlier."

"My husband, Vance."

Tori pleads the fifth with a long swig. They talk more, all along counting down the time for them to retire to their rooms, even extending the curfew twice because the conversation is so good. They're so gone off the wine, each glass is a new stunt. Tori holds her glass up and says, "The good book says God helps those who help themselves, and I'm helping myself to another glass – God help me."

Raquel remembers, "Oh, that's right. You don't know yet."

Tori halts all humor. "Know what?"

"I'm not a believer."

Tori's wowed silence breaks with a casual, "To each his own. I'll spare you the scriptures."

Raquel braces back in her bar chair. "Really. So, you're not about to tell me how I'm going to burn in hell? Or better yet, do the passive aggressive thing and say you'll pray for my soul?"

"I wouldn't be a good Christian if I did."

"You see…" Raquel's pointer finger shakes at the thing Tori possesses that puts to shame every Christian that has judged Raquel for her beliefs. "…that's what I'm talking about – that right there. More of them need to be like you, Tori."

"I wouldn't say all that," Tori raises her glass, advertising the vice that proves Raquel wrong.

Raquel looks down, hesitant to let go of her words and unsure how it might go over, but, "That phrase, 'God helps those who help themselves…' It's not in the bible. It sounds biblical but that quote can be credited to Algernon Sydney, who wrote it in an article titled Discourses Concerning Government."

Tori gives a side-eyed appraisal. "But you know what's

funny? I ain't never met an atheist that didn't know the bible. It's like you all can't just *not* believe. You have to thoroughly know what not to believe."

Raquel says, "I can't speak for everyone else. Me: I'm a preacher's daughter. I've been force-fed the bible all my life by a father who couldn't live by it himself."

They look at the time again and sigh in exasperation. Tori finishes her glass and gathers her purse. "Ok, for real this time. I going back to my room and get me some sleep, girl."

Raquel also stands but stumbles. Tori catches her elbow. "Looks like somebody needs an escort." The pair walk leaning on each other for balance, laughing all the way to Raquel's room door.

Raquel tries to slide the room key in the thin slot but is failing miserably like she would fail a field sobriety test in her present condition. She stops. She presses her fingers on her forehead as if she has a headache. It's not her frustration with the room key, it's something else, something immensely personal, surfacing out of nowhere. Raquel begins whimpering. Tori who has motioned to walk away, stops and returns. "Are you ok?"

Raquel's head shakes no. She is not ok; she's even worse than not ok. She's huffing and hyperventilating. Tori takes the room key. She opens the door and ushers Raquel into the room and sits her on the bed, rubbing her shoulders. "What is it, Raquel? I know you don't know me from a can of paint, but maybe you should tell me anyway. It'll be good just to get it out, whatever it is." She pities Raquel for not having a God upon which to lay her burdens.

Tori hands Raquel a Kleenex from the dresser. Raquel pulls a sheet and dots her eyes as she begins telling Tori about the church shooting, her father on life support, and her regret over their embittered relationship – a relationship Raquel thought she had all the time in the world to fix,

"This happened Sunday and I'm just now crying."

Tori rubs her back. "Hey, everything happens on its own time."

Raquel stands and tremors as if she could shake away sadness like wet on a dog. "I'm sorry to dump all of this on you. I'll be alright, Tori. Really."

Tori stands too. "Are you sure?"

Raquel reaches out and drops a heavy hand on Tori's shoulder. "I'm sure," Raquel says, but her words mean something else; her eyes mean something else.

Tori doesn't look away. Nor is she surprised. She had spotted the sexual attraction ever since Raquel mentioned her husband.

Raquel comes halfway and pauses, feeling an ambush of desire. She asks, "What's happening?"

Tori sees how this married woman needs a teacher, as she once did, so Tori obliges. Tori directs her without a word. She pulls Raquel's hand to her lips. She kisses the palm, and watches Raquel's mouth fall open. She takes an underhand grip of Raquel's chin to bring her lips forward to hers. The kiss is open-eyed, yet sweet and maternal, albeit drunken. Tori smiles, vindicating Raquel, showing her that she has kissed a woman and the world is still right-side up, that she has answered her desire and she is still strikingly herself, or more herself now than ever before.

Their next kiss is more intimate, Raquel, braver this time. She kisses Tori like she kisses Vance, yet she cannot fathom this cosmic vibe that now envelops her, even while swaying in it. She draws back. Her chin lifts as she tries to comprehend her stimulation, like standing in a shower of lust. Raquel tests the lips again and learns that the first surge was no fluke; again, her pores tingle, and the uprising is still amazingly there, roused by the touch of a woman, embellished by the flick of tongues and their pelvic grinding. She checks the dresser mirror and sees that it is all real.

Tori gets behind, tongues Raquel's ear and cups her breasts. Her hands travel downward, digging into Raquel's skirt. Raquel is a nervous but obedient pupil, testing deeper waters, trusting this woman she's met only today. Tori's hand is wise, it knows Raquel's flower better than she does. The fingers curls into Raquel and she tenses and moans; she can't contain herself. Her head tosses back and they shuffle, Tori clutching Raquel with a one-armed grip that is tight and muscular. Tori whispers, "It's alright, baby. It's alright."

Raquel wiggles against Tori, calling the whole thing off, yelling, "No it's not! No, it's not alright." She reels away and stumbles and lands sitting on the bed.

"Says who," Tori challenges.

"I'm married," Raquel says and then buries her face in her hands.

"But you're living a lie."

"This is nasty. This is wrong."

"Wrong? Sinful, you mean?" Tori waits on a response; none returns. Tori leaves her with this: "Who told you this is nasty? Huh? You say you're not a believer, but as long as you let them tell you who you are, what's the difference?"

It's not a matter of them; it's him: Raquel's father, Simon L Bonneau, the man she's lived to defy, somehow operating behind the controls of her subconscious. What just happened indeed felt sinful; she could never hurt Vance. Raquel vows to keep this desire small inside of her, drowning it in both motherhood and in the very deep, but tame love that she has for her husband.

Raquel throws herself back on the bed and watches the ceiling, which begins spinning from her many glasses of wine. She wants to get up again but her head suddenly weights a ton. The ceiling spins like a time warp into the past, into a memory she can't un-remember:

Raquel was in her childhood bedroom with her friend from private school, Emma, the witty friend who had swearing parents and three older sisters who'd give her intel about sex and boys. It was a sleepover. Emma had smuggled in contraband, her book bag open on the bed, bearing a makeup kit, R rated films for the laptop's DVD drive and a few mini bottles swiped from her parents bar.

They watched Player's Club, an action drama chronicling the lives of strippers. They venture to role play, dirty dancing in their patterned panties and training bras. They stopped everything for the kissing scene. Emma asked, "You ever kissed a boy before?"

The thought was so foreign to Raquel, she couldn't even say no because it would imply that she wanted to but couldn't. Raquel asked, "Have you?"
Sinisterly, Emma nodded yes.

"How was it?"

A kiss was something Emma couldn't explain. Why, a kiss is something that must be demonstrated. Raquel went into her old toy chest and handed Emma a doll. Emma laughed and said, "Come here stupid." Raquel stood before her, playing clueless all the way, even after their lips had come together. Simon was listening outside the door, hearing what sounded like a forbidden movie playing. He burst through the door, expecting to catch them watching a rated R movie, but to his surprise he found the unthinkable: daddy's little girl, kissing with that Emma girl, like they were lovers. Simon was incensed. He took his rage out on Emma, running her into a corner with name calling: "Whore! Hussy! Bull-dagger! Trying to turn my daughter out! In my house?!"

He saved Raquel's chastising for after Emma's parents came and disgracefully took their daughter away. Simon then came in with a leather belt. He beat Raquel like an insolent slave, attempting to flay every impurity out of her flesh, "Vile! Unnatural! Unholy! Irreligious!"

Raquel's mother jumped in and Simon shoved her down,

which is the only time he'd ever laid hands on her, for which Raquel still blames herself. Raquel's younger brother, Charles, bucked up to his father in defense of his mother. Simon clamped his only son's throat and shoved him to the floor with his mother. The whole family was down at Simon's feet, yet he still wasn't done with Raquel. He worked the belt until one arm grew tired and he switched hands. Raquel kicked and screamed and cowered. She did all she could do to keep him from turning her into one big, pulsing blister; she grabbed the belt. For that act of defiance, Raquel's doting father struck her across the face with the back of his fist.

Throughout the following days he'd sit her down, not to apologize, but to explain his actions and how he did it to save her soul. He told her, "You are not your own. You were bought with a price, therefore honor God with your body." He used The Holy Bible as his proof. He quoted Genesis, God made them man and woman. Leviticus 18:22 man should not lay with man as with a woman – adding, nor vice versa. Corinthians 6:9 Do not be deceived: neither the sexually immoral, nor idolators, nor adulterers nor men who practice homosexuality will inherit the kingdom of God. Raquel has since amassed a trillion reasons for not be-lieving in God, but her father's beating and the so-called man of God's subsequent justifications, is the one reason from which all other reasons stem.

FRIDAY

For I Am God

RAQUEL wakes looking at the floor. She's halfway off the bed, her blood circulation settled in her face. She is still woozy. She rolls over, scans the room for her phone, sees the television remote within reach and turns it on just to see the time, but ends up seeing more than just the time. She sees something she never would've expected.

It's nearing five a.m. The TV, set to a twenty-four-hour news network, its graveyard shift repetition of earlier broadcasts, thus, repeating the breaking-news interruption covering a second casualty in the Huntsville church shooting; the pastor of New Birth Baptist, Simon L. Bonneau has died. Reportedly, the family pulled the plug late in the night and the pastor was unable to tell his lungs to breath.

Raquel's father is dead. The realization won't take, even though he's been just inches from dead for a week. "Why wasn't I notified," Raquel yells, at the anchorman. Why wasn't she at her father's bedside squeezing a hand at the very moment he passed? Raquel locates her phone and unlocks the screen. She was never called. Bianca – the only person with authority to pull the plug – purposely shut Raquel out of her father's final hour – while Raquel was at a hotel being intimate with a woman, doing the very thing that changed she and her father's relationship forever. "Damn you, Bianca!" Rage gives Raquel a shot of energy, although she's woozy from a rough sleep and from last night's alcohol. Raquel snatches up her keys and purse.

Her tires squeal out of the parking garage. She is headed to her father's home. She decides against calling ahead. Raquel has the security gate's code and the house key; she prefers the element of surprise, appearing at Bianca's bedside, whacking her with a pillow and cursing her out.

It is morning but still as dark as night. Raquel takes the back road to avoid the traffic lights and police; she's speeding. She's guns down the dark highway through a corridor of never-ending pines, holding eighty around curves. Bianca's betrayal gets uglier the more Raquel thinks about it. Raquel is so upset that she has convinced herself to hold Bianca responsible – not the shooter – for her father's death. Her knuckles tighten over the steering wheel; her eyes are a panther's. Raquel's Equinox leans into the curve, its headlights slicing through pitch black, swathing across the walls of trees.

On her right, she sees a pair of headlights inside of the curve, a car oncoming around the bend – but on second look, Raquel realizes that the sparkling orbs are not large and faraway but small and close. And it has antlers. The buck springs. The brakes' scream shatters the fluid world like glass, its hurling shards flashing images. Raquel sees, in detail, the deer's velvet muscled hindquarter, flexed from the leap, it's white cotton breast under its outstretched neck; the horned buck, in the headlights' beam, gleaming like a celestial beast. Raquel swerves, but still clips its back legs. The vehicle launches over the embankment and into the forest. The pine tree's neck snaps at impact. The shockwave sends birds bursting up into the night sky, as if the treetops had sneezed.

It's pitch black under the canopy of trees. While the birds circle back and settled on their branches, their fading calls uncovers the hiss of engine steam and the metallic crackle of cooling metal.

Raquel wakes to the smell of gas. It is so dark that her eyes open and she thinks they're closed. She tries to move, and her left hand feels like a pin cushion. She imagines, but cannot see, that her hand has broken through the clear plexiglass over the speedometer.

Her eyes begin adjusting, her environment shapeshifting through variations in blackness, and slowly she sees a lesser darkness that is in the shape of her white purse. Hopefully, her cell phone is still inside, she thinks, but Raquel discovers that she can't reach the purse because she's pinned to the driver's seat by the weight of the dashboard in her lap. She's trapped and she hears gasoline trickling, its smell growing more rancid; she can't go methodically about this escape. She must hurry and it must first start with her freeing her left hand.

Raquel has to contort her body at a specific angle to even attempt to free her hand, and when she does, the pain is excruciating. Her guess is that her hand is not only cut up but fractured too. Raquel screams as she pulls. She imagines her flesh peeling with each effort, but the gas: she'd rather lose a hand than her life. She pauses just to give herself a break from the pain. She pulls again, screaming as the hand rakes out of what feels like a briar patch. She's able to lean over to dig into the purse and take out her cell phone. She's down in a valley of trees; there's no signal. The smell of gas reminds her she couldn't afford to wait on help anyway.

The car could explode at any moment.

She feels like one of those illusionists or escape artist,

chained underwater in a glass box, an ice pick as their only tool. Raquel is folded up in a six-ton gas-leaking vehicle, a fireball explosion imminent, a cell phone as her only tool, which she uses as a flashlight to assess what she must do to escape.

Raquel puts her body in positions she never imagined. She rings her neck far right against the airbag pillow, she lifts her right shoulder and has to hold it there, but then has to focus on her left foot, turning it outward and lifting up between the seat and the dash. She kicks and barley makes contact with the door. For a better angle, she slumps over the console, the hump is like a knee in her ribs. She kicks again and again; it sounds like soda cans crushing. She hears a thud.

The door has fallen. Judging by the stench of fuel, Raquel imagines she has under a minute. She musters the power to heave upward to release the weight of the dashboard so she can inch under. She has to muster the strength again and again, each monumental effort moving her only inches at a time. The closer she gets, the further the glass shards on the seat scrape blood lines up her back. She screams in pain but must keep going. She thinks of her children, she thinks of Vance, and by comparison, the pain is reduced to a mere discomfort.

She emerges triumphant. She runs to a safe distance and collapses in the foliage, relieved, but then she uses her phone as a flashlight to see her injuries and can hardly find any. The hand that she thought was pouring blood, has just a few superficial scratches, blood not pouring but merely sitting in the crevice of the scratches. The scratches on her back barely dot blood on the back of her dress. She shines the light from her cell phone on the wreckage and sees what looks like: a crumpled candy bar wrapper. "How?!" She looks inside the mangled vehicle to ensure that she isn't still inside – that she isn't her own spirit gazing upon her physical death. The car is, in fact, empty, when she should be in there, red with blood. Dead.

There must be a logical explanation, Raquel thinks, as she's struggling up the incline back to the highway. She spends an hour thinking about it as she walks down the dark road toward the nearest gas station. She doesn't call 911; she'd be inviting a stay behind bars on a DUI. She still has alcohol in her system.

She walks – troubled by the wreckage she shouldn't be walking away from. She researches fatal accidents on her phone and the captions detail, in some cases, complete families dead from cars left in better condition than her own. But she can't trust visuals; Raquel needs numbers. While walking along the pitch-black highway, Raquel researches her car model and crash statistics. She downloads manufacturer manuals. She researches design patens and crash results for her vehicle's specific year and model.

She opens her Uber app to schedule a ride. Raquel is less than five miles from Bianca but has lost interest in confronting her wicked stepmother. She types in the address for the University, which is only halfway between Huntsville and home; she needs a chalkboard.

It is not yet six in the morning when Raquel is walking across the university's dewy courtyard. She has a key to the math, science and physics building. She goes to the classroom where she would normally teach her first class if she wasn't out on bereavement. Raquel has her phone displaying her research in one hand and the chalk in the other. She begins her equations at the top left corner, knowing she'll fill the chalkboard by the end of it.

As the chalk scrapes and taps equations on the chalkboard, Raquel whispers along: "The momentum possessed by… the moving object (p)… equals the product… of the object's mass (m) times velocity (v)… Then there is the impulse momentum change… the base of the tree, of course, didn't move an inch… therefore… it deflected all of the energy back into the car." Raquel stands back and looks at what she's done so far. "Next," she says. "The body of the vehicle and the amount of impact that the design could withstand. Raquel refers back to PDF documents she downloaded during the long, dark walk to the gas station and on the Uber ride here.

Raquel comes to a point where she wipes the board clean. "No. No. That can't be." She's made an error somewhere. She starts over. She works the chalk down to a nub. Tears stream down her face and tie under her chin.

Raquel is scribbling the equations, thinking about the night before, thinking about Tori, her dead father, his abuse, the leaping buck, the mangled car that should've crushed her to death. Raquel circles her final answer, turns her back to the chalkboard and slides down into a sitting position where she hugs her knees and sobs. Above Raquel's head is the circled answer to how she escaped the jaws of death with only a few scratches. It reads: GOD.

A DREAM COME TRUE

Finally, the switchboard operator gives Scoop the answer he's been waiting on. There's no visiting hours for Bishop Simon Bonneau because there is no Bishop Simon Bonneau at the hospital. Scoops leaves early. He wants to catch the grieving wife before the visitors crowd her home. Scoop knows where the home is. He remembers from the night he followed Bishop Simon and was about to confront him but had changed his mind at the last second.

Scoop finds a locked gate, but the closet-sized booth just inside of the gate is unmanned. Scoop checks left and right and then proceeds to scale the gate. A cobblestone road winds up a steep incline between two rows of sycamore trees. Once Scoop scales the incline and stands at the opening of Sycamores, he sees what the inclined earth and tree-tops are hiding, and he gets the feeling that he must've climbed here by beanstalk. The cobble stone road wraps around a waterspout in front of the home. The home is ten times what Scoop imagined; it is homes on top of homes, with its cluster A-roofs and too many windows to count. Mountainlike, its morning shadow blankets the estate. Even a small inherited portion of this life would still be heaven on earth compared to what Scoop is accustomed to.

Bianca is up. The doorbell chimes like steeple bells. She is alone in the massive house; the help has been away all week. Bianca lie on the couch in her house robe, languishing the death of her husband, for which she blames Levi, who is the reason Bianca went to the hospital late in the night, to deny Simon the chance to wake up to a convicted felon claiming paternity for the only child she bore for Simon, the son that Simon was determined to do what he failed to do with Charles, to guide Tre to his inherent call to divinity.

The doctor and the chaplain tried to talk Bianca out of it. The bishop is a man with a family and a local celebrity, yet she's pulling the plug in an empty room. Those close to him will feel insulted. They suggested waiting until she gathered the immediate family, at least, but an impatient Bianca stamped her feet and yelled, "Pull the damn plug, I said!"

The doorbell rings again and Bianca remembers that there's no one there to answer the door but herself. On her way to the door, it hits her. No one should be at her door at this hour. No one called in advance. She was ambushed the day before by Levi, and she wouldn't put it past him to suddenly show up at her home unannounced. Bianca grabs a heavy brass candle holder and breaks the wax candle against the marble floor to reveal the sharp end, pointed like a fencing sword. She marches to the door full of rage, not even thinking to check the surveillance screen for the front door camera. She swings the door open with the five-pound pointed candle holder raised, but the man at the door is not Levi. It's…

She sees Simon backing away with his hands up, speechless. Bianca drops the deadly candleholder. "My good Lord!" She runs to him, saying, "I'm not going to hurt you. I thought you were..." Still the man stands there, dumbfounded. He has resurrected as a younger version of himself. Having Simon back is, literally, a dream come true – the same dream she shared with Will and Ameena at the hospital, where Simon appears and makes love to her. Bianca says, "Don't just stand there. Come inside. You're home."

Scoop is taken aback by this woman's hospitality; still he wants to get right to business. "Just by looking, you probably can tell who I am, and why I'm here."

"You look so good," Bianca caresses his face. Scoop, getting back on topic says, "About the inheritance –"

Bianca puts a finger to his lips. "I'll get it all taken care of. Promise you, I'll do right by Raquel," Bianca says, but then she's hit again by the realization that she's standing there, talking to the man who's vitals flatlined just last night. "I just can't believe that you're here. You read about things like this in the bible but to actually be in it?" Bianca comes for a kiss. Scoop tenses, denying her. Bianca explains, "I did what I thought was right. I pulled the plug *because* of the inheritance."

She slips inside of his guard and kisses him. She holds his face to her lips, lips as soft as butter. Skip has never felt hands so tender – nothing like Shay's hulk fingers. Bianca's hair smells like jasmine, like royalty.

Scoop is well aware that Bianca has mistaken him for his father – her husband – but he doesn't correct her. He doesn't say a word to jeopardize an opportunity with a woman whose kiss just put fire in his loins. Being with this woman would be everything that the going-through-the-motions with Shay isn't. Shay, he could hardly look at. Bianca, he can't stop looking at her. Bianca leads Scoop to Simon's bedroom. They stop to kiss some more at the foot of the colonial style canopy bed. Bianca asks, "How long will you be here?" Meaning in the physical form, before heaven snatches him back.

Scoop takes it as a question of performance. He licks his lips and says, "As long as you need, baby."

Bianca grabs him by the collars and pulls him down on top of her. They roll around under the covers, tossing out articles of clothing and then the moment arrives. Scoop is on top of her. He pulls back from the kiss and digs under the cover, maneuvering. Bianca's eyes pop and she gives a husky, "Oh God."

Scoop smirks, as he remembers how Simon was described to the lawyer. Scoop says, "Ain't no beanie weenie over here, baby." And there Bianca was, just one day removed from county jail and a mental institution, now mounted by her husband's bastard; reveling in what she believes to be her second coming.

HAVE YOUR WAY, GOD

Ameena, Charmaine and Rose hear a mighty rumbling outside. Ameena hurries out to the porch with her hands on her head as if she's keeping it from falling off. Motorcycles cover the driveway and the lawn, idling like perpetual thunder.

It's Will and the Holy Roaders. The bikes are so loud, Will has to lipread when Ameena yells, "What're y'all doing?"

The men cut the engines. Will comes forward with some sort of sash laying over his outstretched arms; a cameraman trails him. Will calls Rose, who steps out from behind her mother and grandmother, a hand covering her mouth. Will reads from a note in his palm, a speech that speaks for himself and the bikers behind him. "On behalf of the Holy Roaders, Rose, I present you with this sash of courage, for you being positive and resilient throughout this trying time.

You and your mother made the very tough choice to turn in the stolen money, setting an example for what it means to be a good Christian. You had the faith to do the right thing and to believe that God will provide. It's what we believe. And we, The Holy Roaders, being a vessel for God to provide through us, we are glad to inform you that we're throwing a fundraising parade in your honor. We will raise that money back for you, and we're going to send you off to Disney World, or wherever you want to go." The Mimms women run down the steps and hug Will and the bikers hug them. Even the toughest looking men lift their sunglasses to wipe their eyes, or wipe tears with their pocket bandanas.

They congregate in the yard for a time, even neighbors join in, but before everyone disperses Ameena must leave; she has a rehearsal to go to. Will tries to talk her out of it. The fugitive is out there. Ameena argues, "But he's not a threat. He tried to help us."

"He wasn't on the run, then. You turning in that money is what led to them charging him. It's different now. You're actually not safe."

Ameena says, "I have to do this." She plants a kiss on Will's lips and backs through the crowd to her mother's car. Even while driving she's thinking about Will… That sweet, wonderful Will, Ameena thinks, as her head shakes. Ameena can't get over the thought of him. She can't shake the feeling that when she kissed his lips just back there in the yard, that she was kissing the lips of her husband.

The whole ordeal doesn't really hit Ameena until she's driven well into the city. She thinks about all the bikes on her lawn, the recognition they bestowed upon Rose, the upcoming parade in her honor, and Ameena is suddenly over-whelmed with warmth, with joy. God has answered. Ameena looks up and says, "Jesus." That name strikes a heart chord. Ameena echoes a softer *Jesus*. The tears begin. The name swells in her throat, so she must say it to breathe again, *Jesus*. She whips the car off the street and somewhat into a parking space. She's saying *Jesus, Jesus, Jesus*, all along. Her voice alone can't pour out what's building inside of her. Ameena gets out of the car and trots out on the side-walk just in time for the Holy Ghost to take hold. Her hands shake in front of her as if she has burned them. Her feet shuffle and hop in place; her head thrashes about and her crying eyes are closed shut. Over and over again, Ameena repeats, "Jesus, Jesus, Jesus, Jesus." Pedestrians frown and skip past her. One appears to be calling the po-lice, but four black women come busting out of a beauty parlor, one in rollers, another's head is frothy with lye. They join hands around Ameena to contain her, and then let the Holy Ghost have its way. They encourage it. *Yes God. Have your way Father.* Ameena bends forward thanking God and then throws her head back, thanking Him harder. The women stay with Ameena until she pipes down. The don't ask what breakthrough she's received nor about the hard journey leading up to it. They know God for them-selves – know that when you look back over your life, how a gratitude so overwhelming can spark from within your bones and shake you. They recognize the Broadway ac-tress, but do not ask for autographs. Ameena waves them off, assuring them she's ok. Ameena sits inside of the open passenger door, her feet resting over a street drain, where she runs her hand back through her hair and takes a deep breath before getting back into the driver's seat.

When Ameena arrives to the rehearsal venue, immedi-ately she can tell something's wrong. The director, Dimitri Dalton, stops mid conversation and trots over to her.

"Ameena! I was calling you!"

She could've missed the ring for a number of reasons: the roaring bikes, her front lawn crowded like a yard sale, or her sidewalk Holy Ghost. "Is there something wrong?"

D'mitri points and says, "Meet Pastor Lynn Stewart, the play's author."

Ameena turns and extends a hand, which the woman doesn't even notice.

Lynn says, "I hear you're friends with Bianca?"

Ameena rears back slightly, frowning. "Well, um…"

"I need to get in touch with her. Bianca is in danger."

This oval faced Lynn in serious. Her full brown eyes are dead set on rescue. Ameena offers Bianca's phone number but Lynn says, "You call her." Before Ameena could dial, Lynn tugs her and says, "Come! We might already be too late."

While on the way to Lynn's car, Ameena's second call fails. "We haven't been on good terms. She's probably ignoring my calls."

"Or we're too late," Lynn says.

They duck into Lynn's Lincoln sedan. Ameena says, "Do you mind telling me what's going on?"

Lynn replies, "You've read the script, haven't you?"

"Yeah."

"Well, Bianca is the real-life Shannon. And the real-life Troy just came to Huntsville, looking for her; his real name is Levi."

Ameena's head shakes as if to toss out the woman's unbelievable. "No way that stuff really happened."

"It did." So, Troy, or rather Levi, had tried to murder his wife, so he and Bianca could be together. He had drugged his wife and tied her up in the basement while he dug her grave in the forest, setting a large basin in a recess in the ground and filling it with high concentrated hydrochloric acid, in order to vaporize her into thin air, flesh and bone, gone without a trace, but it was Bianca who was privately pregnant with Levi's baby, that rescued the man's wife, Nay, from that basement.

Ameena points and says, "Take a left here and then go straight for a ways." They talk more on the way to Bianca's house while Lynn fills Ameena in on the events that occurred beyond the play's end. Bianca was rumored to have been pregnant for the married Pastor, Levi Ginyard, when she left South Carolina without a trace, or a note goodbye, her apartment still full of her furniture and belongings. She hadn't since contacted anyone, not even her own parents. Lynn explains that no one knew where Bianca was until they saw her face on the news concerning the church shooting. Levi spent eight years in prison for the kidnapping and the attempted murder of his wife who was Bianca's best friend.

To clarify, Ameena says, "So Bianca got pregnant by her best friend's husband…" Ameena thinks about the script and it feels like too much to have happened in one place: the Ponzi scheme, the pastors battling for the pulpit, the pastor-involved shoot-out, the attempted murder and rescue, the pastor falling for the women's rights activist (Lynn) whose presence challenges the patriarchal church's lesser-vessel culture. Ameena asks, "Lynn? How long have you been a pastor?"

"About ten years."

"So, you're… You're Gail, from the play? I always thought the name was a bit small for such a strong character."

"The name is a play on symbolism. It's Grail minus the r. Grail, as in Holy Grail, the symbol for womanhood." Lynn swats a hand, giving up on the explanation. "Not that anyone gets it. Only other writers, I suppose."

They pull up to the gate and ring the bell. There is a camera pointed at the driver's side window, and a speaker where Bianca's voice flows through, saying merrily, "I know that ain't you, Lynn? My God, what a surprise!" The gate slides open. They ride slowly over the cobble stone road, and when Lynn sees the home, she says, "The church that my husband Dana and I co-pastor is bigger than New Birth, yet our home isn't even *half* of this."

Before the car comes to a stop, Bianca is outside, brimming with anticipation. The two greet each other like old sorors. Bianca is so happy to see Lynn, she's even willing to tolerate Ameena. "You got my shoe, heifer?" Bianca kids.

On the way in, Ameena and Lynn look at each other, exchanging reads: awfully jolly for a fresh widow. Bianca glances, nearly catching them. "Lynn, you come all this way —"

"— To warn you, actually. Levi knows where you are. He's coming to Huntsville, if he's not here already."

Bianca's head cocks. "You talkin' bout Levi? I *talked* to Levi already," Bianca swats. "Ain't nobody worried about that man."

Lynn asks, "Do you think Levi came all this way just to talk?" Lynn adds, "Catfish contacted me, thinking I knew how to get in touch with you. He told me that Levi wants his son, and he's not leaving without him. If you're standing in the way, he will try to get rid of you; that's just who he is."

"Since when have you started listening to anything Catfish has to say? How is Levi supposed to get rid of me?" Bianca waits to be humored.

"This is a man who has burned down one church, broke into another, and tried to murder Nay. What won't you put past him?"

"Lynn, I'm not about to sit here and waste my breath talking about Levi." Bianca crosses her ankles; her hand swats limp." So how have you been, girl. You and Stew...

How many children y'all got?"
Lynn sighs and answers. "Three."

"Three!"

"My first born, King, is ten. You and I were pregnant at the same time. I just didn't know it. And then there's the twins, Adelle and Carter."
Bianca makes praying hands and says. "I'm so happy for you, Lynn."

"Thank you, Bianca." Lynn scans the massive home, her brows raised. "I'm Happy for you too."

Bianca leans forward as if letting Ameena in on a secret, "You know Raquel? She nearly died this morning." Bianca leans back, nodding as if the near tragedy vindicates her.

"Raquel, your stepdaughter," Ameena says, in astonishment, but also to revealing, to Lynn, Raquel's identity. "Well, where is she? Is she hurt bad? Is she in the hospital?"

"Police called me around ten thirty this morning. Said they found her big ole SUV balled up smaller than a sports car. She left the scene. Showed up later at the college with only a few scratches. That's where her husband, Vance, picked her up."

"Praise God," says Lynn, even though she doesn't know Raquel from a can of paint.

"Say those words to that ole atheist and she'll give you a mouthful. Vile thing."

They go silent momentarily. Bianca's behavior has them bewildered: upbeat despite a just-dead husband and seemingly disappointed that her stepdaughter's accident was only near-death. Lynn covers their silence with, "I'm so sorry about your husband, Bianca. My condolences."

Bianca clasps her hands over her knee and leans back, eyeing the two, unsure if she should entrust them with her secret, but she tells anyway. "Keep your condolences, Lynn. Condolences are for the bereaved." Bianca watches her visitors go deaf, *What? Huh? What are you saying?* "I am not bereaved. Because Simon is not dead. He was here just this morning." Bianca waits on them to try to detain her and haul her back to the psyche ward. Between the three, not a muscle moves. Bianca adds, "Remember, Ameena, the dream I told about when we were at the hospital? It came true. Every last detail –"

"– Oh, God." Ameena lets out, not of excitement but of disgust at the thought of Bianca romping with the dead not long before hugging her guests.

Lynn offers, "And you're sure this wasn't a dream – a really vivid dream?"

"I have bite marks, if you wanna see it." Bianca reaches in her bra, pulls out a white bow tie and twirls it on her finger. "He left this."

Finally, Lynn asks the obvious, "Bianca, are you sure you're ok?"

Bianca's face dims. "Am I ok... As in what?" Bianca posts a palm to hold off their response while she laughs. "You think I'm nuts? I just passed an evaluation that says I'm not – I'll have you know."

Lynn presses her temple with four fingers. "Look, I'm not trying to argue with you."

Bianca shakes the bow tie in her fist. "You can't argue with this. Where do you think I got this? Huh? And if this bow tie isn't enough to convince you, I can bring you our soiled sheets."

With that, Ameena and Lynn get up from their seats and begin backing toward the exit, their hands raised, clean, and determined to stay that way. Bianca yells after them. "Just you wait and see! He said he's going to reappear at church on Sunday. Three days later, he will rise again.

Lynn shoots back, "That was Jesus! Not man!"

On the drive back to the rehearsal, Lynn vents. "People are supposed to mature and grow, and not repeat the mistakes of the past. Absolutely nothing has changed about Bianca except her age. I've seen her like this. If she would fixate on God like she fixates on a man, she could be a leader of many." Lynn hammers the steering wheel with her fist. A few minutes go by and a call comes in that Lynn scrambles to pick up. She covers the receiver and whispers. "It's the police." Lynn had called the police to alert them that Levi, a convicted felon who came all the way from South Carolina to Huntsville Alabama in search of the woman who thwarted his murder plot a decade ago, but the officer reports that there is nothing they could do to Levi. The man has done his time in prison and is no longer bound by parole. He is now a citizen. He can travel as he pleases. Free country.

YOKED

Shay's got a new dress and wants to show it off. She holds the hanger to her body in front of the dresser mirror. She's twisting and eyeing herself as she speaks to Scoop. "Let's go out to the Hot Spot tonight?"

Scoop is in bed. He turns over from his side to his back and says, "No, I don't wanna go to the Hot Spot tonight."

Shay tries to sell him on the idea. "Everybody gets in free before eleven. Plus, they got ten-cent wings."

"So," Scoop dismisses.

Shay tucks the dress under her chin, freeing her hands to hold up matching earrings. She locates Scoop's eyes in the mirror. Staring him down, Shay says, "If you agree to go out with me tonight... when we get back? I'll give you that thing you like." Shay, eyeing his reaction, can see his loss of appetite. Shay suspects that he's actually done it. Not just flirting with another woman, but that he's been with one. She couldn't possibly guess that it was a millionaire preacher's wife; Shay suspects Chandrika. Shay turns sinister. "Tell me, Scoop, did you always like it like that, or did you acquire that taste in prison?"

Scoop springs out of bed and begins putting on his pants. "I better get outta here before I knock the hell outta you."

"It'll be your first time and your last."

"Just because I don't wanna go out for ten cent wings, you insult my manhood? What couple thrives on ridicule? That's *your* normal. And I'll be damned if it becomes my normal. See: you not just in the slums; the slums is in you."

Shay looks at Scoop in such a way that looks past everything he just said. "Who is she?" It's the only thing that matters to Shay. "They told me how the other day when you went to Mike-mike house to play dominoes, lo and behold, that Chandrika was there, sittin' on your lap."

"*They* said what?" It's almost comical to Scoop. "Put a name on it. Who is they?"

"The same *they* that says Chandrika got the claps."

Scoop's head pokes up through the neck of the t-shirt that he pulls down over his body. "Anybody worth listening to, would be spending their time talking about how to get out of this hell hole. Only the small-minded wastes time gossipin' about other people."

Shay is turned to the window, checking on her children in the courtyard at play, running through the clothes hanging on the line. Shay comes away from the window and goes to her nightstand, saying, "Y'all dudes come outta prison thinkin' y'all so intelligent. Ain't read a book before or since." She pulls the red devil mask from the nightstand and throws it on the bed. "But what good is *talking* different when you can't *do* different?"

The sight of that mask snatches the life-force out of Scoop's body. His legs give and he lowers into a squat beside the bed.

"Uh-huh," Shay nods. "You robbin' churches now?"

"Shay," Scoop says, woozily.

"Frontin' like you ain't got no money. Probably givin' money to Chandrika hoeing behind."

"Shay."

"Don't even wanna go out with me. Don't even wanna touch me, seem like."

"Shay!" Scoop stands.

Shay pulls out her phone, her thumb ready to dial. "I'm finna get my cut! Or your black ass is going directly to jail. Do not pass go. Do not collect two hundred."

Scoop dives across the bed and swipes for the phone. "Gimme that –" He misses. By the time he's back to his feet, Shay is out of the bedroom. Scoop gets his gun, tucks it under his belt and storms out front. Shay is backing away, still threatening to dial. "Where's the money?"

"There *is* no money, Shay! That money was turned in yesterday. You haven't heard?"

"*All* of it was turned in?"

"All of it."

"Nah, nigga. I know you. Why would your selfish behind rob a church and give all the money away? That ain't in you."

Only the truth would make sense, but Scoop can't tell her that the true robbery is not of the collection plates, but of Bishop Simon's estate, or Shay would use the evidence to extort half of it for herself. "It was guilt, Shay. Guilt. That's why we gave the money away."

"You think I'm playing?" Shay shows him the phone screen as she dials 911.

"Shay. Stop!"

She puts the phone to her ear and says, "Hello operator?"

Scoop draws the gun in silence, his face menacing. Shay sees the demeanor of a killer who, all this time, has been living under her roof, eating at the same table with her children. This dwelling, she has used as leverage to keep him, he has now made her the prisoner within it. Shay tells the operator there's been a mistake and she hangs up. Shay chokes up on the brink of tears. Scoop holds his aim and puts the other hand out, its curling fingers silently asking for the phone. Shay clutches it to her breasts, crying, "I shouldn't have to ask you about the money, Scoop. We're supposed to share everything. We're supposed to be together. How could you do me like this?"

Scoop eases closer. "We'll discuss all that later, Shay, but right now, all I'm concerned about is you giving me that phone."

"Why?"

"So, we can talk." Scoop stuffs the gun in his pants.

"No."

He eases closer. "Shay? You pissin' me off."

Shay retreats. The back of her leg bumps the couch arm and she stumbles. Scoop sees his chance and pounces. They're wrestling for the phone, Shay blocking him with her back to him, Shay screaming for some concerned neighbor to hear. *Stop it! You're hurting me!*

The tussle escalates to domestic battery. Scoop cups his hand over Shay's mouth to pull her head back, grunting with effort as he says, "Where you think you going huh? Huh?" And then, "*Ow!*" Shay bit his hand. He snatches it back and shakes it.

Shay uses the space to throw her butt back into him, with each thrust, yelling, "Get! Back! Get! Back!"

Her eldest son, Lil' Rick, runs in. He screams at Scoop to leave his momma alone. He gets a two-handed grip on Scoop's wrist that Scoop can't shake off, so he closes his fist and shoves it into the chest of the screaming boy, who falls back, gasping. The other kids rush in to see the horror, the youngest, Imani, wailing as if she's witnessing the death of her mother, who is facing the corner, wheezing and slobbering in Scoop's sleeper hold, but hearing the cry of her daughter, Shay resurges, growling with effort as she bulls back, forcing Scoop halfway across the room. Lil' Rick is back on his feet. Scoop cannot see the oldest son, but he hears the boy say to his siblings, "Watch it, yall. Watch it!" Next Scoop hears the swoosh of the aluminum bat, which clocks him on the side of the head with a loud, metallic ping. Scoop's eyes roll up into his skull and he falls stiff like a toppled statue.

A lot has transpired since the metallic ping on the side of Scoop's head. Scoop wakes hog-tied, 'Bama style. His hands are tied; his feet are tied, and then the hands and feet are tied to each other. He's on the floor lying on his side, facing Shay's thick ankles. He wonders if she's called the police. "Shay! What did you do!"

"You'll find out directly... puttin' yo hands on me – you done lost your damn mind."

Lil' Rick gets a running start and punts Scoop in the butt so hard, the impact jars his own glasses uneven.

There's a knock at the door. Scoop fears it's the police. Scoop wiggles and thrashes like a caterpillar overtaken by a troupe of ants. Shay steps over Scoop and is humming whimsically as she goes to answer the door.

It is not the police; it is Gene and Big Mike. Bike Mike doesn't wait to be asked in, he barges in, wearing his red track suit and matching Roll Tide ballcap. He looks down on Scoop, the son who has went against everything Mike has taught him. "So, you a killer, Moses?"

Scoop is still hogtied on the floor, turned away, his eyes locked at its corners to fix on Mike, to sass him. "Maybe y'all should blame yourselves for *naming* me after a killer." Mike rewards Scoop's insolence by digging a foot in his behind with an effort that makes Mike bite his bottom lip, his front teeth bearing under his gunslinger's mustache.

Scoop cannot see, but hears Gene, who can't get past how badly she was deceived. "You had me all up in that lawyer's office, sharing things I never wanted to share with another living soul. All along, you had *blood* on your hands? The only thing that's keeping me from turning you in, is the fact that you're my son."

Gene and Mike's disappointment tugs at Scoop's insides, bringing him near tears. When Scoop speaks, his voice cracks and comes out young, like child who used to bring Gene crayon drawings. "I did it for *you* mom." This time it's no drawing; it is a murder.

Shay doesn't get it. She doesn't understand how robbing the church, but then stuffing the money in that actress's garbage can, helps Gene at all. There's more money left, Shay gathers. She doesn't know about Bishop Simon being Scoop's father, nor the pending inheritance.

Mike points at Shay, but asks Scoop, "You put your hands on this woman?" This betrays everything Mike has taught him about being a man.

Scoop also hears the voice of his mother say, "As a couple, ya have to talk things out."

Like a giant injured bird, Scoop squawks, "Couple!"

Shay chimes, "I didn't have to call them. I could've just turned your behind in – sent you back to prison."

"*You're* my prison."

With that comment, Mike quit, and turned to leave, but three seconds into walking out of Scoop's life, he pivots, and turns back confused. "How is you the one with all the mouth, Moses? You're the one in a position of weakness, right now. How many times have we talked about this: play from the hand life deals you." Mike begins untying Scoop, adding, "Shay ain't robbed no church; *you* did. You don't have nothing on her; she's got something on you. That's the hand you got, Moses. So, your only play to keep yourself a free man is to find out just what it is that Miss Shay, here, needs from you, in order to keep her from going to the police."

Shay looks down and around. She looks at her hands. She knows what she wants, but she is ashamed to say. "I want what you got, Scoop. I don't have this…"

"Don't have what?"

A tear slips quicker than her blink can catch. "A family… You got people to call. You got a mom and a dad who loves you; who took the time to raise you and teach you right from wrong. You got a daddy," which is the exception – a trophy – considering Shay's housing project upbringing. "My daddy pretended like I didn't exist. My momma was on crack. My momma spit in my face one time because I accidentally walked in on her and one of her Johns." Shay feels the spotlight on her and doesn't know what else to do under it than talk, tumbling along the tragic soliloquy of her life. "Every day my momma told me how she hated me. She somehow got it stuck in her head that daddy left her because of me – and not her addiction. My daddy didn't want me neither. He took me to his family reunion one time, and no one said a word to me. I just sat there with everybody looking at me like I was some kind of zoo animal. My mom was in and out of jail, but not always for the drugs. Mainly for fights. That's where I got my temper. She never got over my daddy. She'd try to run interference on all his relationships. She tried climbing in through my dad's girlfriend's window and that woman left a meat-knife standing in my momma's chest. So, I moved in with daddy and that same girlfriend. Soon after, daddy packed up and left me with the same woman that killed my momma. She didn't want me either. But from the age fourteen to eighteen that's where I was. She said the only reason she kept me is because she put me in that position by stabbing my momma – not that she actually cared. When I was sixteen, she told me she was going to put me out at age eighteen, so she said I better get pregnant so that when I turned eighteen, I could get food stamps and housing. And that's what I did." Only silence could respond to such a tragic life.

Five, six beats pass before Scoop lets out a somber, "Damn,"

"Damn," Mike seconds.

Scoop then turns an eye to Shay. "But we was talking about what you wanted, Shay. What do you want?"

Shay breaks down, her cries too overwhelming to allow a reply. Gene comes alongside Shay and holds her. Holds her like the mother Shay never had.

Mike tells Scoop, "Let's me and you go talk for a minute." Scoop leads him to the bedroom.

Mike goes in first and stands at the door like a guard. Mike looks Scoop square in the face, waiting, examining. Scoop can't make him out. Scoop shrugs. "What, pops? Dang…"

"Put it together, Scoop. You don't know what she's asking you?"

"What she needs to do is just come out and say it. All this beating 'round the bush," Scoop pouts.

"It is impossible to truly ask for something you don't feel worthy of."

Scoop just turns away, his fists on his hips.

"You really don't get it?" Mike's head shakes. "She wants marriage, son."

Scoop's jaw drops. "Say what? Aw hell naw. Ain't no way pops." Scoop paces like a caged tiger. "Ain't no way."

Mike brings his hands together by the slots of his fingers. "Marriage is a bond, right… It's a bond that's, honestly, more about loyalty than love. You two are already bound, forever, whether you like it or not. What you did, killing that preacher, and Shay's knowledge of it… She can forever use your freedom against you. Be grateful that she's only using it to keep you with her."

"I can't do that pops. Ain't no way. I'll take prison first."

"So, you prefer your right hand over a woman? You'd

rather share a bedroom with a hard-up, stank foot dude over Shay? Think rational, Moses. Or maybe you *didn't* do it for Gene, like you said."

"I did… For you too, dad."

"Well, if you tick Shay off and she turns you in, you can't inherit nothing *to* share with Gene or me. So, stop acting crazy, son. There's no way you can think that you can just up and walk away, leaving Shay in this dump while you collect that inheritance, get yo'self a big ole house and fine new chick… A woman scorned will turn your black ass in, just for spite. You can't lie to facts, son."

Scoop identifies the bars still all around him. Bars with no shape or form, yet inescapable like the bars that held him captive for six years. Scoop's cry is powerful and quick, like a passing thunderstorm. Seconds after collapsing into Mike's arms, Scoop is backing away, wiping his eyes with the heels of his palms.

"Come over here." Mike calls Scoop to the dresser. "This'll go over much better if it seems like it's your idea." He opens Shay's trinket box and pulls out a ring.

"C'mon, Mike. She knows I'll be doing this just to stay out of prison."

"She already knows that what's keeping you with her now is her roof over your head and her food in your belly –"

"– Only because you kicked me out."

"I didn't kick you out, Moses. I gave you two options: to get on a job and to respect my house *or* leave. You chose." Mike stirs a finger in the trinket box and finds a better ring, the closest thing to an engagement ring he could find and hands it to Scoop. "Here. You know what you gotta do. Now, let's go back out front, man… Funky in here."

They go out front and Scoop gets down on one knee, even giving a little speech about how much Shay has done for him – to make it seem genuine. "This was always going to happen," Scoop insists, even though this feels like a child's forced apology. "I mean… You may have never felt like somebody's daughter, but you gon' feel what it's like to be somebody's wife."

This marks the happiest day of Shay's life. She comes away from the embrace, glowing, but doesn't attempt a kiss. Mike assures her that Monday morning they're going down to the Justice of Peace to get them married. Shay is grateful, she hugs Scoop again with this news, her embrace pinning his arms to his body. Lil' Rick is confused; he is the only child there. He had escorted his brothers and sisters over at the neighbors while Shay had hogtied Scoop. He doesn't yet know how to explain to the others that their mother is choosing the man that just tried to kill her, to be their daddy.

Gene weeps for her son. She comes over and touches his face. "Y'all gonna need God. Moses. Shay. Get yourselves churched. Get in fellowship with people who know the way." She sees her son's stress and says, "Without God – in the midst of this?" Gene turns away her head shaking, their God-less future too grotesque for words.

Scoop's only consolation is that, in due time, he will have all the money he'd ever need in this life yet be chained to four children and a woman who makes him sick.

THE HOT SPOT

Shay insists that they celebrate. Scoop thinks, *celebrate my life sentence*. He could use a drink. They go out to The Hot Spot, after all. They just make the deadline to get in free, which is a relief because they only have enough money for a few drinks and a shared basket of wings. The Hot Spot is a hole-in-the wall club dressed up with a wall couch and a strobe light in the ceiling that hangs like an ornament. There's a large, unpainted rectangle on the wall where an industrial sized refrigerator once was; this building used to be corner market.

Scoop doesn't realize how badly he's dressed until he sees the drug dealers, with their gold grills, and crisp designer threads, posting up at the bar, luring women with drinks. Scoop makes a mental note to return after he's gotten his inheritance, to put them all to shame.

Scoop is impressed at how well Shay cleans up. She now looks like the pictures she used to send him in prison. Still Scoop has to employ a mind trick to make her appealing to him, since they'll be man and wife come Monday. Scoop tries focusing on her candy red lips without seeing the jowls under her chin, or admire her long thick eyelashes without seeing how her beady eyes sink into her swollen face, or if he could focus on the switch of her wide bottom while she walks in front of him, but train his eyes up when facing her to avoid the sight of her belly – do these things and then maybe, Scoop figures, he won't feel like running away screaming every remaining day of his life.

Shay pulls his hand, guiding him toward an open table, where they sit. Chadrika is there. Shay says, "Your girl, Chandrika over there, lookin' *real* hard." Shay suddenly can't keep the woman's name out of her mouth. Shay goes on about how Chandrika really has two children, but her oldest is being raised by her grandmother. Chandrika must be on crack, Shay determines, because of how she's birthed two children and is still as skinny as a teen. Shay goes so far down Chandrika's list, she even commenting on how her baked macaroni is garbage, even though she cheats by adding packet cheese sauce.

Scoop says, "Now, I now know where that jealousy of yours comes from."

"What're you talking about?" Shay is delighted to know that he's being perceptive of her; it says he's paying attention.

"Your mom. Wasn't she jealous of all your dad's girl-friends?"

"Scoop? I didn't say anything in that living room that I want repeated. I'm going to tell you this last time. Don't talk about my momma. I don't talk about her."

"I figured if you realized that you're trapped in her generational cycle, you might wanna –"

Shay drops a fist on the table. "Do not talk about my momma, okay? If I wanna talk about how that hoe over there was jumped by three women for sleeping with each of their men and now has as an ugly scar down her right thigh, which is why she doesn't wear short skirts, then let me talk about that. It gives you no right to bring up my momma."

Scoop notices how each time, Shay cuts her eyes at Chandrika and next leans forward to talk about her. "Shay," Scoop says wearily. "If you're gonna sit here and talk about the woman, can you at least not make it so obvious? You keep messing with Chandrika if you want to. She's a real one, Shay. She crazy."

Shay, not to be bested, even in theory, replies, "Let her run up. I'll show her crazy."

Scoop reaches out for her hands, asking, "Let's focus on us. Can we do that? We got a whole future in front of us and you sittin' up here runnin' your mouth about that chicken-head over there?"

Shay takes the advice. They begin talking about their future. Shay admits concern over their marriage disqualifying her for housing and welfare.

Scoop still keeps quiet about the inheritance. "We'll be a'ight," Scoop assures, nonchalantly. Shay excuses herself; she goes to the restroom.

Chandrika, as if dying for this window of opportunity, b-lines to Scoop, her club walk, an overdone imitation of a runway model. She tries to get him to dance, to give Shay something to see when she returns, but Scoop won't leave the booth. Chandrika stamps a high heel on the floor and folds her arms, pouting, "Why do you even mess with her." She comes closer to hear Scoop's response over the music. She leans forward and slicks her hair from over her ear, seductively.

Scoop shows her his palms, smiling bashfully, "I told you, it's complicated."

"Let me make it easy for you. Come with me. Leave with me, right now."

If Shay didn't have the power to send him back to prison, Scoop would have taken that upgrade in a heartbeat; his face shows it. "Chandrika, all we had is one good evening together, and we ain't even do nothing. All we did was talk."

Chandrika's head lowers as she giggles. "Maybe you don't understand me. What I'm saying is, go get your clothes, come stay with me until you get on your feet. I know you don't want her."

Maybe if there wasn't loud music, they could hear Shay stomping towards them. Shay stops and drops a limp hand in front of Chandrika's face, to show off her engagement ring. "Obviously he *do* want it because he surely put a ring on it!"

Scoop is trying to slide out of the booth to get between them, but Shay swings her butt around to block him.

Chandrika is so startled, her lower body had started retreating before her upper body. Once she's backed down to a safe distance, Chandrika scoffs with her eyes fixed on Shay's hand, "A ring from a gumball machine?"

Chandrika should've been watching Shay's non-ring hand, the hand swatting like a bear's paw. Chandrika's late effort to duck makes it worse. The heavy-handed smack sends her sprawling awkwardly, skidding into a sitting position against the bar, where Shay crowds her before she could get up. Shay stomps Chandrika like a roach that won't die – stomps her between the legs and then her chest and face. Shay backs away gloating in victory, egging Chandrika to come on and get some standing up. Patrons close in, ready to break up the fight until they see Chandrika rising to her feet, screaming with a box cutter raised high.

Shay is the last to see. She sees the flash of the blade only after it struck through her windpipe. Shay coughs. Blood spurts from the red line across her throat. She gurgles and drops forward on her knees. Chandrika runs through the crowd towards the exit. No one detains the woman with the box cutter.

The women are screaming, people are running. Scoop screams, "Shay!" There is nothing Scoop can do to help her. "Aw, Shay!" He is sad for her, for being murdered like her mother, not only by a blade at the hands of another woman, but also, like her mother – a victim to her own insecurity. Scoop cannot celebrate his freedom from marrying her, nor the death of one, out of three people in the world who knows he killed the bishop. If given the choice, he would've chosen the prison of marriage over watching Shay die. He runs for the exit like the others, as if he has no connection to the dying woman. Scoop runs because he knows the police will be on the scene, and he doesn't want to be around when they get there.

SATURDAY

Second Thoughts

THEY'RE at the Sounds of Summer Concert Series. It's been a long week, with the church shooting; Will nearly choked to death; the bishop expiring from his injuries, and Ameena learning that her monster is not only out of prison but has stepped foot in her yard. The concert becomes their world away from everything. They are there for each other, not so much the music, but last on the program, there is a rapper, Dizzy D, that Rose is a fan of.

This may be the last concert of her life, so she milks it for all it's worth. She dances; she Googles the lyrics and sings along with songs she's hearing for the first time. She goes vendor hopping; Will is paying. His budget has no end. Everything that Rose looks at and then refuses, Will buys anyway, like beaded bracelets, a drink-holding straw necklace, a corn dog, a hand held fan with streamers, photo booth pictures, and suddenly Will rushes them back to the front as Dizzy D comes to the stage where Rose cheers for the little-known rapper as if he's Beyoncé.

A few songs, in, Dizzy D cuts the music with a knifing hand. He silences the audience for an announcement. He calls

Rose by name. He leans at the edge of the stage, scanning, still asking for a girl named Rose. Rose looks back at Will and Ameena with her mouth open, her eyes full of wonder. Will shoos her, "You hear the man calling you." Will knows she's the right Rose; he arranged this. The Holy Roaders president's wife is on the free summer concert committee. Rose hugs Will, and the hug sticks. She hugs him like a father, believing their relationship is the closest she'll ever come to having one. Rose hears her name again and breaks away. Will hurries her along and watches proudly as Rose takes the stage.

Dizzy D announces that Rose has cancer and speaks of what he's been told about her courage, and her positivity throughout. He urges the crowd to support next week's parade that will be held in support of her. Next he has Rose signal the band and he says, "Me and Rose... We gon ride this song out together!" He delivers the hook and then puts the microphone under Rose's chin for her to repeat. Rose even adlibs, going on her own, high-stepping and raising the roof. The crowd adores it.

Will is hit both a joy and sadness that caves him in. He folds his arms to contain it. His lip trembles. He hides his tears behind his large fist. Ameena, too, is ruined, as she watches her little Rose having the time of her life. Ameena's head just shakes as she says to Will, "I don't deserve you. I really, really, don't deserve you." Will tries to correct her, but words are unavailable to him; he fears trying to speak and having his raw emotions spill out like a horse's neigh.

All day Will has had a secret in his pocket. Part of him questions whether it's too soon. But he's known her for a whole year, answers another aspect of himself. But then a different voice – still his own, but a more pessimistic version, counters, but we've only reconnected for but a week.

For Will, the whole loud concert is drowned out by the paranoia of his thoughts. Will eyes Ameena from the side, watching her cheer for her baby, but he sees her differently. He knows this woman has secrets. What did she mean by saying she doesn't deserve him? Was that her just saying things out of gratitude, or was it a window into her subconscious? Will's present uncertainty makes a fool of the man who went out yesterday morning, shopping that expensive engagement ring. Suddenly, Will's feet feel cold and he isn't too keen on getting his pant knee dirty.

It worries Ameena, keeping Rose out of the house this long, but surprisingly she's fine; she is still full of energy by the time Will's car pulls up in the driveway. Rose goes in the house, leaving Will and her mom sitting in the car to discuss things they can't discuss in front of her. Will has been saying all day that it's not safe for them to stay where Lonnie knows they will be. Will had been offering Ameena to have herself, Rose and Charmaine stay at his home until Lonnie is caught; Will offers again. Now that Rose isn't around, Ameena can directly explain why she's been declining the offer all day. "Rose is on borrowed time. Rose's next sick bed would be her last. When she leaves here, I want it to be in the comforts of home – not over at her mother's boyfriend's."

Will says, "What I'll do, then, is run back to my place to get my things. I'll sleep on the couch, just in case Lonnie returns."

Ameena touches his hand and thanks him.

There's a few beats of silence and then Will smirks, "Boyfriend, huh… That's what I am to you?"

Ameena squints. "What?"

"You just said it. You said you didn't want Rose getting sick at her mother's boyfriend's house."

Ameena tickles his chin. "You're my *man*, Will, and even that adjective falls way short of what I really feel for you."

With those words, Will is certain that if he presents the ring the answer will be yes.

Will takes a deep breath and says, "I hope what I'm about

to ask you doesn't rub you the wrong way, Ameena, but...
We're in a relationship, so I feel like I have a right to know.
The detective told me some things that were being said about
you and Simon –"

"– Like what? By who?" Ameena says, as if she's ready
to round up all the gossipers and give them a piece of her
mind.

Will takes her hand and asks, "Why can't you just tell me
what happened?"

"I've already told you that *nothing* happened. All you have
to do is believe me over the rumors." Ameena was done, but
something else occurred to her. "– And if you can't do that,
what are we doing?"

Will looks her up and down, saying, "If nothing happened,
why can't you explain what that *nothing* was?"

"So, you think I'm lying to you? Look, stop this, Will. You
have just given me one of the best days of my life. Let's leave
it at that. I don't like where this is going."

"If that's your answer, Ameena, I don't like where this is
going either."

Ameena's head turns quite mechanically, stopping once
Will is square in her sights. "You know what," she smirks,
even. "Believe whatever it is you've heard, ok? The heck
with it."

Will looks away and covers half his face with a hand. He's
too ashamed to even look at Ameena when he counters, "I'll
tell you what I *do* believe. I believe that you took off your
clothes the very first time you stepped foot in my house."

A switch flips on, in Ameena; her eyes burn with maniacal
intensity. She shoves Will. Shoves him again, tears sparkling
like diamonds in her eyes. "I did that for you because I love
you. And now you wanna turn it into something else?"
Ameena thrusts a hard finger up between them to stop his
reply, warning, "Don't come back. Not tonight." Ameena gets
out, slams the car door and speed-walks into the house. Not

once does she look back.

Will sits there, dead-faced. She'd left hanging, the one question mark in the way of Will's proposal. Alone in his car, Will studies the sparkling engagement ring. He finds himself listening… listening to loneliness, which is the surfacing of the sounds you never hear when accompanied by the one you love, like a belly gurgle, the tap of the velvet box as it shuts, the groaning of leather seat as he lifts up to pocket the engagement ring. For the first time today, he hears his engine hum. Will bashes the dashboard and curses himself.

Ameena is on the inside, in her mother's recliner, also cursing herself for not simply telling Will rather than using the moment to test his loyalty, or to vet his willingness to trust her. She could have told him. There's nothing to hide – well, not really, Ameena thinks. Maybe she feared that while telling him, maybe he'd judge her for almost doing the unthinkable, even if, for the sake of her daughter.

Now since the subject was brought up, Ameena can't get that day out of her mind. She takes herself through the ordeal like a tourist in her own history.

She was having tea with Bianca and her other high society church friends. From how they speak with such dignified mannerisms, one would think they're discussing politics, or discussing the future of some philanthropic endeavor, but no. These women look the look, but sadly, do not operate above gossip and rumor.

Ameena did as best she could to pretend to be engaged, to hold her weary sighs and keep her eyes from rolling. She wasn't there for the tea, nor the gossip, nor for the company of high-class hens. Ameena was there for Simon – since she couldn't get him on the phone, nor at the church by appointment – since he was so well-guarded by his staff. She used Bianca's friendship, of which Ameena was already disenchanted with, as her inroad to confront Simon L. Bonneau face to face, to either get help for her daughter, or hear him justify, under God, why her ailing daughter is unworthy of help from a church whose storehouse has millions in surplus.

Ameena asked to be excused. Bianca gave her directions to the restroom, directions Ameena had no intention on following. She hurried through the large home, looking in rooms along long hallways, ascending the stairs.

She found Simon on the second floor, in the recreation room, playing billiards in his silk robe, drinking port wine and talking on the phone. There was a deer in headlight moment. Silence. Just eyes. Simon tells the person on the other end of the phone that he'll call them back, and then he turns his attention to Ameena. "You look nice." He lowers his head in shame and giggles. "Let me stop lying. Girl, you look exquisite, if you don't mind me saying so."

"I've been trying to get in touch with you." Ameena choked up, emotions brimming already.

"You can get in touch with me now." He laid his pool stick on the table and picked up the glass of port wine from the top, his ring finger tapping the rim of the glass.

"Why won't you help my daughter? She has cancer."

"Your sister, you mean?"

"She's my daughter."

He takes a bitter sip and says, "Bianca must not know you up here talkin' to me – jealous as she is. She will not only slap the hell outta you, she'll later go 'round spreading your name like butter on bread."

"I had to. I've tried everything else."

"We need more time to talk than this stolen conversation. If Bianca comes looking, this is the first place she'll check." Simon said, and walked past Ameena, leading her out. "Follow me."

They relocated to Simon's study. He held the door open as Ameena entered. She could've sworn the man sniffed her hair as she walked by. He closed the door behind them.

Ameena walked to the middle of the room, turned and saw that Simon's robe was open, his body bloated and melted with age, his chest hair thick and grey like ceiling fan dust. Ameena swallowed hard.

Simon asked, "So, how much do you need?"

"Our insurance just started over, we still have a ways to go to reach the insurance's catastrophic cap, so everything is still out of pocket. I mean... What can you give?"

"You go through hell and high water to get to me and don't even know what you need?"

"I need anything. I am broke. I wasn't rich, by any stretch, but I was good. This disease has taken everything I had. I sold my car, I –"

Simon waved a hand to quiet her. "Bottom line, you need help, right?"

"Yes." A tear dripped.

Simon snatched a few Kleenex out of the box on the bookshelf. He handed Ameena the Kleenex and then proceeded to embrace her, as if to console, with his open house coat. Ameena was mortified at the feel of this man's bare chest, his chest hair on her lip, like walking into a cobweb. Ameena cringed and shook loose. She used the Kleenex to wipe her bottom lip rather than her tears. "I'm sorry," she said, afraid to offend him. "Caught me off guard."

Simon cleared his throat. "As I was saying, bottom line is you need help, financial help. We can figure out the numbers later, but I... actually, am going to need something from you."

It suddenly became clear to Ameena why the man's robe was open and why he had lured her to a more private room.

"Look, Simon, I'm saying I need help from the church. So, whatever the church needs from me, doctor bills, bank statements, whatever... I can provide."

Simon began tapping the side of his drink with his ring finger. He said, "All I need... is for you to touch the hem of my robe."

Ameena looked down at the hem of his robe which hung as low as his calves. Ameena looked up again, and verified, in Simon's eyes, that he was dead serious. "You are not Jesus!"

"If my money can save that little girl's life, damnit I am Jesus – to you!" Bishop Simon was as serious as Noah. "Touch the hem of my robe," He pinched his house coat and shook the bottom. "You see it down here? You'd have to get down on your knees to touch it. And while you're down there, I'll give you a little something for that smart mouth of yours." In a more sympathetic tone, he added, "Your daughter needs you, Ameena. What will you not do for her?" He came forward and Ameena did not move; she stood there crying, but not retreating. He dropped his boxers and Ameena said, through the grit of her teeth, "You are going to burn in hell."

"Aw, stop all that fuss, now," he said as he ran his hand back through Ameena's hair. He took Ameena's hand and massaged himself with it. "You're gonna do this for me, ok? For your daughter. C'mon, now." He was breathing heavily through parted lips.

Ameena pulled her hand back.

Simon looked her in the eye and said, "Don't get to thinking that you can weasel your way out of this now, and then crawl back later in tears, pleading. Try that if you want to, and that little girl's gon' be one dead lil' bitch – messing with me." He tried to bring Ameena's hand back to his crotch.

Ameena recoiled, both hands drew up to fists balled tight in front of her chest. "Do not touch me again!"

Ameena didn't hear Bianca's high heel steps approaching, but Simon did. The moment Bianca opened the door, Simon had pulled up his boxers, and Ameena had swung with everything she had, slapping Simon with her whole hand. Bianca gasped. Simon's glass dropped and broke, he stumbled back, cursing. He then came forward with a fist drawn back to slug Ameena, but he stepped on a piece of broken glass.

Ameena turned to Bianca, her face already wet with tears. "Your husband just sexually assaulted me!"

Simon hopped around on one foot, yelling in pain, but also explaining to Bianca, "She offered to put her mouth on me! She wants money. Ole black dog!"

Bianca was stuck trying to decide who to believe, and then it dawned on her. "Ameena, the directions I gave you for the restroom didn't say come up the stairs."

Ameena explained, "I did come looking for him, but –"

"– About money?"

"Bianca, let me explain."

Simon who had sat in a chair to nurse his cut foot, looked up and said, "You don't have to explain nothing. My wife can look at you and know that I wouldn't want no damn porch monkey like you."

Bianca, with her side now chosen, looked at Ameena and said, "Get out of my house, heifer, before I drag you out!"

The husband and wife marched Ameena out. Bianca had driven her there, and there was no way Bianca was going to drive her back. Bianca even warned her guests that if they offered Ameena a ride, that they would never be welcome in her home again, so Ameena walked. She walked ashamed, embarrassed, and violated. She walked for a grueling two miles by the time Will and his biker friends came roaring.

Rose finds her mother in the recliner and lays across her. Ameena kisses her face and says, "You are heavy, girl."

"Want me to get up?"

Ameena withholds her answer, just to see that waiting look, the twitching of her brows, and her cute mouth pinned closed. Ameena shakes her head no.

Rose says, "Ma?"

"Yes?"

"Are you and Will gonna get married?"

Ameena rolls her eyes, smiling. "If he asks… I don't see why not."

"Maybe he don't ask because he thinks you'll say no. Maybe he'll ask if I tell him you're waiting on it."

Ameena frowns at her daughter but ruins the facade with a smirk. "Why are you trying to marry me off, Rose? I don't know if I'm ready for anyone to cut into our time just yet."

Her daughter knows when her mother is avoiding the topic of death. She caresses her mother's face to let her know that she's ok. "What if I want to be in a wedding before... You know..."

Ameena laughs out loud. "Me? Make a lifelong commitment just so you can play dress up?" Tears fall, but it's not altogether sadness; she actually considers Rose's request but offers a more doable solution. "Why don't we find a ball to go to – that way, we can dress you up like a princess without me having sign my life over."

The daughter weighs the idea in the drooping corners of her mouth and decides, "That'll work."

The doorbell rings. Ameena feigns exasperation. "I bet it's Will."

Rose asks, "Do *you* wanna get the door instead?"

"I'm mad at him, right now." Ameena smiles mischievously and gives these instructions: "Tell Will that I'm not dressed; therefore, there is no way in *hell* that he can see me tonight."

Rose hops off the recliner, antsy to participate in the game, but before she darts off, she turns back eerily. "Are you sure you want me to say h, e, double-hockey-sticks?"

"This once," Ameena anoints, with a nod. "But promise you'll say it like you mean it."

Rose turns the porch light on and pulls the door open wide, fully expecting Will, but it's not Will. It's a dark, bald headed man who waves gently and asks, "Is Ameena home?"

Rose comes away from the door to go poke her head around the corner to call her mother, but looks back and sees that the man has welcomed himself in. Rose hurries toward her mother, thumbing back over her shoulder, yelling in a whisper, "There's a man in here."

No sooner than Rose says it, Ameena sees the monster who has entered their den with his hands up, saying, "I only want to talk."

Ameena scrambles up from the recliner to shield rose and she screams. Lonnie begs, "Why did you give away the money?"

Ameena screams again. "Get out!" Charmaine comes running with a lamp raised, looking for who to bust over the head. She nearly drops the lamp where she stands when she realizes it's Lonnie, but then she comes at him screaming. Lonnie draws a gun and stops her in her tracks. Lonnie takes the lamp from her hands and sets it neatly on the ledge of the mantle where the flat screen TV is mounted. "I didn't mean for it to come to this."

Rose calls for her grandma. Lonnie, with a twitch of his gun-hand, permits Charmaine to go join the other two. The three women huddle together on the couch now staring at the monster and the gun. Rose, having death already as her constant companion, she doesn't fear the man as much as the others.

Will is finishing up at a nearby gas station, still thinking about how the argument should've went differently. He didn't get a chance to explain himself; he let Ameena shush him when he had so much to say that would help Ameena understand why he asked the question in the first place. Instead, Will let it go. He reckons it was the respectful thing to do; she's upset. Let her anger run its course until she's ready to listen to reason.

Or not. He's thinking like Pastor Will. Maybe that moment

needed Biker Will. The more Will thinks about it, the more he feels like a chump for being shushed and pushed, and the more convinced he is that he will go back to Ameena's home, tell her what's on his mind, put the ring on her finger and inform her who her husband will be. He pulls out of the gas station, mumbling to himself the things he would say to Ameena.

There's an old pickup truck in the yard when Will returns; maybe some male friend of Charmaine, he figures. The porch light is on and he notices that, oddly, the front door is open. He hears distant police sirens, which uptakes his concern, so he reaches into the glove compartment and grabs the gun that he'd recently taken from his brother. With the gun down by his side, Will approaches the house, slowly, but then he realizes that the distance police sirens are getting louder, squad cars barrel around the curve, coming here. The pickup truck must be Lonnie's. The fugitive on the run has come here for who knows what reason. Squad cars screech to a halt on the street. With red and blue lights spinning across the yard and against the house, Will dashes into the open door, before the first arriving officer could exit his vehicle – Will, easily deciding to take his chances with the fugitive over the police. He stumbles into a scene he could have never imagined.

Lonnie was sitting but has risen to his feet. The women are crying, but not in terror. Ameena's hand is out. "Will," she says.

"Pastor Will," Lonnie says with his arms up, each hand weaponless. "No hostages here, brother."

Ameena asks, "Put away the gun, Will."

This is Biker Will. "You don't tell me what to do, woman."

"No for real," says Rose, who is up on her feet, standing in front of Lonnie. "We're just talking. I'm talking to my dad for the first time in my life." If Rose wasn't dying, she would not have seen this as an opportunity; she would've only seen the monster, like her mother and grandmother. It was Rose who had gotten up from the couch, looked back upon her cowering mother and Charmaine and she had said, "Don't let your spirit be ruled by the flesh."

Rose had approached the man without fear and proceeded to have a conversation. They'd just gotten started talking when Will came in.

One of Lonnie's raised hands pointed down at Rose. "Wise beyond her years – this one."

Will lowers his gun, his head shaking, baffled, lost.

Ameena offers, "Have a seat, hon."

"I'll stand."

Rose sets a look upon Lonnie and asks, "Have you asked God for forgiveness for what you did to my momma?"

Lonnie's head slumps forward, and he pinches the top of his nose bridge to trap his tears. "Every day of my life," he cries. "There were times I tried to take my own life but couldn't," he whimpers. "I was a fugitive then, like now. I knew I was going to prison for a long time. I was mad at the world for the situation I put myself in. And I took it out on her…" It's all the words Lonnie could manage. He's trembling, as if *he* is the hostage and Rose, his captor.

Rose asks, "If you were mad at the world, you could've done anything to anyone. Why a child who wasn't responsible for anything you've been through? Why rape?"

"Because I'm a coward." He chokes up and backs away, his hands waving away too many demons; too much pain.

"I guess what I'm trying to ask is: who hurt *you* in that way?"

Lonnie uses the hem of his shirt to wipe his eyes and nose. "My cousin… I was only seven… He held me down…" Lonnie began bawling like the child he was when he was raped.

Ameena's head shook, refusing to see her rapist in any light of victimhood, refusing to see his rape passed to her like some sort of baton. "You can sit up here and cry and sob, but it still doesn't change what you did. Did *I* go out and rape someone because it happened to me?!"

Rose turns to her mother and says, "The question then, momma, is how did that violation manifest in you? What sins has it enabled in your life?"

Ameena can't muster a challenge to the dying daughter that she denied for fourteen of her fifteen years of life – the baby Charmaine wouldn't let her abort. Ameena's eyes are blurry and warm with tears, as she revises her past. Tragically, she had to learn, at a mere age of twelve, how to disown her own body; the only way to survive rape without losing her mind. Her first experience with sex was an act of power, a power that was taken from her, a power that with every subsequent encounter, she has tried to win back. In her career, she's disowned her body to use it as currency, conceding it to men of power, so they'd surrender portions of their power to her. In Simon's study, Ameena, desperate to pay for Rose's chemo, nearly put her trust in exchange of her body, rather than trusting God, and that is why Ameena feels like God punished her with Rose's terminal diagnosis. Ameena now feels the weight of her chains and it buckles her. They say forgiveness is freedom. Ameena doesn't know this for herself, but out of desperation, she looks at Lonnie and begins anyway, "I heard you speak… And I believe you regret what you've done. But you need to know what you've done to me. Every failed relationship…" Ameena looks down and shakes her head. "Because of you I became a guarded, emotionally unavailable, and manipulative…" Ameena is coughing and sobbing but powers through what she must say. "I left God because of you. I tricked myself into thinking that I was living life on my own terms. I kept six states between me and my daughter because every time I looked at her, I saw you!" Her face tightens and she seems she couldn't stand on her own. Will tries to comfort her but Ameena holds him off and looks Lonnie in the eyes. "You talk about yourself going to prison. What you did put me in a prison. I will be dealing with it for the rest of my life. Even though you've put me through hell, in the name of God, I forgive you."

Lonnie drops to his knees with his hands together in prayer as he cries out to the lord.

There is not a dry eye in the room. Rose hugs Ameena, looks into her crying eyes and says, "You're free now, ma. You're free," Rose says. Ameena holds her daughter tight, apologizing to her for ever leaving her, and the girl becomes heavy in Ameena's arms. Ameena pulls back to look at her, but Rose slips from her grasp and hits the floor, her eyes closed, like she's having a pleasant dream. Ameena drops on the floor over her daughter. It has happened. Charmaine and Will get down on the floor with her. They're all shaking her and yelling her name, but the girl does not respond.

Lonnie covers his face and wanders out of the room; the girl's death weighing heavy on his shoulders. Lonnie stands in front of the door, one hand on the knob, the other pulls the gun out of his waist. He runs down the steps with the gun drawn and shots ring out like a battle zone. Lonnie trembles like he's hit with voltage. Bullets pelt the home, breaks windows and flowerpots on the porch. His truck lowers from shot tires. The gunfire doesn't cease until he is lying on the lawn motionless.

Inside, Ameena and Charmaine blanket rose, and Will blankets them. Even though the shots have stopped no one dares to go outside. They stay where they are. An officer comes, one eye closed, aiming behind the sights of his gun. There's already an ambulance outside, called in advance. He radios for a stretcher, believing the young girl was hit.

Will stays with the police to give a statement. Charmaine and Ameena get into the back of the ambulance to ride to the hospital. Will could hardly stand on his own two feet, much less recall all the details for their police report.

They rush Rose to Huntsville Hospital on Sivley Rd. Ameena and Charmaine run alongside the gurney until nurses tell them they have to turn back. They turn and go to the waiting room where they have a mini wake of just two members. They talk about how courageous Rose had been, and how she is a light and an inspiration, how she'd be smiling on even her sickest days. The others in the waiting room hush and pretend like they're not watching. One walks over and offers some words. A young woman with long braids keeps telling her child to be quiet and sit still as if her child, both healthy and quick, mocks the two women who has surely suffered the loss of their own.

An hour later, the doctor comes out with a clipboard tucked under his wing. He removes a pen cap from his mouth and puts it back on the pen. "Ameena Mimms?" He is the hue of a peach stone, his forehead slopes early, which gives him a perturbed look. "I'm Doctor Bynum. We actually go to the same church." Ameena and Charmaine are slow to get up, the doctor puts up a signaling palm. "You might want to stay seated."

With that, Ameena and Charmaine prepare to mourn. Whatever explanation this man has is nothing more than babble to the fact that Rose is dead. Dr. Bynum doesn't wait for their cries to wain, he speaks at it, listing everything that Rose's condition is not, "At first we thought maybe it was a medicine-induced stroke, but her blood pressure was good. We thought maybe she'd fainted, but she would've awakened on the ride here. She'd lost consciousness and we couldn't explain why..." He then hooked his fingers inside of the stethoscope hanging around his neck and says. "God has been known to do that..."

Ameena and Charmaine realize that with all the man has said, Rose's death hasn't yet been pronounced.

"Just like God put Adam to sleep in order to remove the rib out of his body —" The man's volume is growing louder, as if not to pronounce death but rather to proclaim life, his pointer finger now pointing at heaven as he adds, "Like Adam, God put your precious girl to sleep in order to reach inside of her body, and pull out her infirmity. Cancer is no longer in Rose's body; it's in God's hand!"

Their hands are on the cheeks of their stunned faces, as if they were slapped from all sides. The doctor aped them, freezing himself in that same stunned pose, his mouth open like a capital o.

"Noooo," Ameena bellowed. "No cancer?" She glitched twice; she's panting. "No cancer?"

The doctor's hands cross in front of him and then knifes out to full wingspan like a baseball umpire; his call, a re-sound *safe*, "*No* cancer!"

Ameena is bouncing and giving praise, her arms swinging like she's fanning flames around her.

The doctor isn't done with the good news. He watches her with his arms folded, a hand coming out of the fold with its index finger hooking his nose. He then hops into action, say-ing, "Let me show you something Miss Mimms." The man peels his coat back and struts. Rose is in the distance. He takes Rose's hand and leads her to her mother, the doctor commanding, "Take your daughter! Leave this hospital! Yall don't have no business here! Rose, you will go on to marry, have children – ha! *Grand*children. God ain't nigh done with you yet!" Doctor Bynum, and the women have a Holy Ghost party right in the waiting room area. Hopping in place, arms swinging, thanking God loud enough for every ear to hear. A nurse claps her face to cover her tears. The waiting room comes alive, smiles and tears, like an early Sunday worship.

A HOME

Scoop can't find a home for the kids. They surround him

as he sits on the couch, his head as heavy as an anvil. Their closest living relative, their grandfather wouldn't let them step foot in the door. "What I'm supposed to do with them kids." The man's daughter died, and this is the only concern he had. He offered to bury Shay and no more, as if it's a favor. Shay has a cousin, the only other relative that Scoop knew existed. The cousin, Lolita came to the door scratching. She seemed willing, but a few minutes into the conversation Scoop turned leery. Lolita had no questions about the children's well-being. She wanted Shay's food stamp and bank cards. She has two children of her own who looked malnourished, the girl's hair thick and tangled, the son's shoe missing a tongue. Scoop took the kids, saying he'd be back with the bank and food stamp cards, knowing he would never release those kids to the care of a crackhead.

Scoop knows that Child Protective Services wouldn't be able to place four children under the same roof; the kids would be split up. The children surround him as he sits on the couch. The little one sitting on the floor between Scoop's legs, still doesn't understand death; she thinks her mother has simply forgotten to return home. Little Ricky, who just one day before had crowned Scoop with a metal bat, now leans on him, looks to him, trusts him; he is all they have. John points to the elephant that's been following them all day from house to house. "*You* can keep us."

They all huddle together and hug, but the children are unsure if the embrace means yes. Scoop makes grilled cheese sandwiches and Ramen Noodles for dinner. They sit in front of the television. For a moment, things seem normal, but then the news interrupting the regularly scheduled program to report that the second member of the New Birth Baptist robbery was shot dead in a standoff with police. Scoop learns that, aside from his parents, he's the only person alive who knows who killed Bishop Simon. His eyes turn glassy for Old School. Scoop remembers, after the robbery, Old School was leading him down the path, telling him about an inheritance other than the one from Simon Bonneau's estate. He remembers walking the path that he couldn't see, and Old School telling him he's on the path whether he can see it or not. It just now dawns on Scoop that the path Old School referred to had little to do with their trek through the woods. Old School was religious. He took all the money just so he could give it away to the actress with the sick child. Scoop had promised Bianca that he would come to church on Sunday but had no intentions whatsoever of showing up. Now he feels like he needs church, like his mother, Gene, advised. He needs it to understand what to do with this inheritance of four motherless children.

He needs to go alone. He'll leave the children with Gene where they all will live temporarily until Scoop receives his inheritance. Scoop finally answers them, "Y'all mines. I'm gonna make sure y'all have a future."

There was no way that Ameena could spend the night in her mother's house where a man was just slain on the front lawn. She brings Charmaine and Rose with her to Will's home to spend the night, her suitcase hurriedly stuffed like a packed mouth. They all sit up late, talking, lifting up God in prayer and in conversation, in light of the miracle he has bestowed upon them. Life's journey is reimagined; all the tragedy softened with the knowledge that, all along, the journey was headed towards triumph. All while, they sit and talk in the living room, Ameena holds onto Rose for over an hour. Ameena only lets Rose go when she has to use the restroom. Will points Ameena to the closest one, in the master bedroom.

After leaving the restroom, something on the dresser catches Ameena's eye. Next to Will's keys sits a small velvet box. Her heart stops. Ameena forces herself to walk on past it, but she stops and looks back. She can't leave the room without knowing what's in it. She opens the box and the diamond engagement ring takes her breath away. She puts it on. It's a tight fit, but it fits. She puts her hand out at arm's length, splaying her fingers. She then places her hand over her heart, posing in the dresser mirror, dreaming an image of Will behind her as her husband. She thinks about their argument after the concert and realizes why Will wanted clarification about she and Simon's history, and now she sees the magnitude of dismissing his concern. She hopes Will hasn't reconsidered, but the only way for her to know is to put the ring back in its box and wait however many excruciating days until he plans the perfect time to pop the question – or not.

Ameena is so caught up in her thoughts she'd failed to realize how long she'd been gone. She tries to put the ring back in the box, but she can't get it off her finger. She claws the ring and pulls, but it's stuck at the knuckle. She bends forward, elbows out for a mightier pull, but it only hurts her finger, the metal against bone, the knuckle skin piled like rubber bands. Ameena hurries back to the bathroom, wets her finger and spurts it with hand soap. She hears Will call back, "You alright in there?" Maybe he heard the commotion. She hears him coming and the ring seems ready to give, but she's afraid to break her own skin.

The bathroom door is open. Will comes in with the empty velvet box in his hand and sees Ameena with a wet blouse and soapy hands and he says, "What the..."

Ameena looks up, confused, not knowing what else to say other than, "Yes..."

"Yes?" Will comes to her, laughing with his arms open to receive her. Ameena cradles his face, soapy hands and all. The kiss transports them into their future, like a time-condensed video, with a wedding springing up around them which quickly melts away, the kiss enduring the light show of many dawns rising, and nights falling, children appearing around them, beautiful each one, their kiss enduring still as their hair's grey fills in like snow fall and they pull away from the kiss with crow's feet around their eyes their deep laugh lines satisfied of the life they've lived, and then time whips them back to this day, smiling, everything they'd just experienced through that kiss is the promise they've sealed with the engagement ring.

Ameena struts out front, patting her hair as a way to flaunt her ring. "Guess who's getting married." Charmaine gets up out of her chair and the women have a group hug.

Will says, "She found the ring in my room and got it stuck on her finger. I wasn't going to ask until I first got your blessing, Charmaine. And Rose, your permission." They adorn the man with everything he asks and more.

There are enough bedrooms for each to have their own. Although they're now engaged to be married, Ameena goes upstairs to sleep in the same bed with Rose, and Will goes alone to his bedroom.

In the wee hours of the morning, Ameena wakes up and rolls out of the bed. She knocks on Will's bedroom door and he welcomes her in. As Ameena walks into her fiancé's bedroom, she clarifies that she only wants to talk. They slip through the bedroom's glass sliding door and sit on the deck where there's a private view of the large pond. The nearest visible home is all the way on the other side.

Ameena then tells Will every detail about what happened that day in Simon's study. Will listens to her and gazes in her face as if lost in her beauty, even without makeup, even in her silk bandana hair wrap she wears every night. As she tells the story, Will holds her hand, his thumb caressing. When Ameena finishes the tale, Will has no reaction. He thanks her for sharing. He touches her face and kisses her in the night breeze, the high bright moon giving her face a blue tint.

Will twitches, as if something just hit him. "I almost forgot to tell you. You're going to be a first lady soon."

Ameena looks at Will like he's crazy.

"I was notified by text that, as early as Monday, they'll be making me a formal offer to become the head pastor."

"But what about Jevon?"

"He's a snake. He spread rumors about you and the pastor. He called the police on me, almost got me killed just so he could preach this Sunday. He did it to himself." Will stops, looks at Ameena and says, "You're not happy for me?"

She remembers. "Am I happy for you…" She throws her arms around his neck and gazes into his moonlit eyes. "Of course, I'm happy for you. It's just that… First lady?"

"What about it?"

"I'm not groomed. I'm not church-ified. I just got back in the church a year ago. And then there's my career."

Will gives her a reassuring kiss. "As a team, you and I will do whatever we have to, in order to make sure that all of your desires are met." With that reassurance, Ameena kisses him good night, leaves the room and creeps back into the bed with Rose.

SUNDAY

THE doors of the church open. Will is already in the preaching seat; Jevon Saunders is nowhere on the premises. This Sunday is seven days after one of the most tragic days ever in the city of Huntsville. Will leans forward, legs spread, elbows resting on knees. He looks intense, like he can't wait to deliver the word God has given him. His content, this time, is not so perfectly structured because no way, after yesterday's miracle, that Will could go with his prepared sermon.

Bianca borrows a microphone from the director of music ministry and then she cuts in on the deacons' devotional praise. The deacons think it odd, but welcome her; her husband has just passed; everyone grieves in their own fashion. Bianca sings just as gay as a bird. *Said, I'll go-ooo, if I have to go, by myself.*

Over the weekend, Bianca had called everybody and their mommas, spreading the word that Simon will rise again like Jesus – the Sunday after his Friday death – as if hence forth there will be a second Easter on the calendar. From the onset of service, Bianca doesn't sit poised in her first lady seat; she is active. Her gleefulness, in the wake of her husband's death, slowly takes on a look that seems unhealthy.

Next, she crashes the praise team quartet's performance with her own boisterous singing, making a scene. The praise team try their best to pretend that Bianca's impromptu is welcomed. Bianca claps above her head in order to encourage audience participation. As the music plays in the background, Bianca explains, "You might be wondering why I'm so happy today when my husband is scheduled to be eulogized on Wednesday. Because I know something you don't, that's why." Bianca paces along the front of the stage as she speaks to the audience. "Do you believe that our God is a deliverer? Do you believe He is still in the business of miracle-working?" The congregation responds yes with their praise. "Amen," Bianca agrees. "So, you'll believe me when I tell you that God has raised my husband, your bishop, up from the dead!" Everyone goes silent. Hands pause mid-clap. Bianca grows a tight, facetious smile and says, "And you call yourselves believers." She mistakes their disbelief in her words as disbelief God's power. "Bishop Simon L. Bonneau will attend this very service, you watch." They cut the song, but Bianca still isn't done. "That's not the only miracle that has happened within my family this weekend."

Will has seen enough of Bianca's foolishness onstage already. He gives her the signal to hurry with a whirl of his finger. Bianca spazzes, in response, whirling her finger back at Will, with ten times the aggression, saying, "This isn't about me, stupid."

She had the microphone covered but it still picked up the insult. Heads turn. Grand church-lady hats dip to their neighbors. Will backs away coughing in embarrassment. He can't set her straight in the middle of a service, despite Bianca acting like she's just busted out of the psyche ward.

Bianca comes down to the front row and takes Raquel's hand. She ushers Raquel forward and hands her the microphone for a testimony. Raquel stands with her feet together. She looks around and then waves. "Hey." She's clearly out of sorts, having to look upon a sea of what she still believes to be judgmental Christian folk. The congregation makes her as nervous as she makes them; anyone who comes before the church and starts off with a hey, rather than a Giving honor to God, is clearly un-churched, and it makes the church hold their collective breath when the un-churched, is in church with a microphone to their lips. "My name is Raquel. I'm Bishop Simon Bonneau's daughter. And if you were not a member of this church before I turned eighteen and shipped off to college, you have never seen my face in this building. There's a reason for that... I have a preacher for a father, but I'm atheist." There's an audible groan among the congregation. One elder's *Aw naw baby*, speaks for all.

"I'm a math and physics professor. We don't believe in much of anything that cannot be explained with numbers, equations or theorems. But even the discipline of mathematics has its gods – each of them now dust in their graves, unable to help me work out any equation, unable answer this question that I have." They perk up at the logical cue *dust in their graves*. It nods to Jesus's empty grave. They begin studying her with anticipation. "That question, I will get back to in just a moment, if you will." Raquel is so overwhelmed with emotion she fans her face, but she gathers herself, tossing her head back to look over the congregation. "I nearly lost my life just days ago. I swerved for a deer. I was going eighty, um... My car went airborne into a wall of trees. It is nothing short of a miracle how I'm standing here, right now, telling you that I got out of that car with barely a scratch on my body." The audience gets up and praises, the drummer starts popping, and the organ reens, but Raquel waives her hands to call off all the gladness. She has more, "You see, I wasn't so convinced. By the looks of that car, I should've been dead, but I'm a mathematician. I needed more than just optics. I had to calculate the speed times the estimated force and check the Chevy Equinox's crash statistics and..." She loses the audience with the details, offering more proof than hardened believers have a taste for. It takes Raquel a full minute to explain the equation and recover their attention. "I think about my child, and my husband whom I love very much." She calls Vance up to join her to stand behind her, although he has yet to be converted. "The biggest fear I had, when I went airborne into the trees, was not being able to grow old with this wonderful man." She grips her mouth and powers through a gust of emotion. "I was talking about a question, remember? That *question...*" she throws a pointed finger forward that makes them rear back in their seats because everyone sees it: her father's conviction showing up in her, the way she paralyzes the congregation with her stare. "That *question*, you may now have guessed, is: how did I make it out of that car alive? Every possible explanation, in mathematics, was ruled out. On Friday, I was an atheist, but today I'm telling you that the only reason I am alive, is God!" Raquel drops the mic, literally, as if she feels its power and it scares her. This former atheist feels what everyone in the congregation has already identified: her calling to preach the gospel. The congregation praises, the band rewards them with energy. Worship is full blown well ahead of the preached word.

Will paces on the stage, stewing with his sermon turning hot in his belly. He dances (he never dances). He raises holy hands and shouts at the top of his lungs. He can yell, but never like this, with eyes so wide they're liable to pop out of his face. As the mass praise calms down, Will is still up with raised front-facing fists, his head lowered, shaking.

When time for the offering comes, the church goes quiet and tense. The previous week this time, it was mass hysteria, kids trampled, a bishop's brain blasted out the back of his head like confetti.

Bianca is nervous the whole time, but not because of last week's shooting. She's awaiting Simon. He said he'd be there; he didn't say he'd be on time. Again, Bianca gets behind the podium in preparation for the offertory prayer.

Again, Scoop walks through the door and there is a loud

scream. Many bolt on reflex, as if it's last week all over again, but at second glance, they stop with one foot raised in flight. There are no robbers. No guns. A young lady screams nevertheless, trotting backwards down the aisle pointing to the entrance, yelling, "Bishop!? Bishop!?"

Chatter boils like a stew. One deacon walks forward, peering, and then the man breaks in the middle, bowing, but peering up. "Is that really you?"

They recall Bianca saying that her husband, their bishop, would be raised from the dead. Half the people up close, seeing Scoop pass through the reeds of people, actually believe that this man in the all-white tuxedo and shoes, might be some incarnation of Simon. He appears to be the same person, but not the same. Those who have been New Birth members since the beginning see the young Simon who founded this church.

Raquel positions herself for a better look, ready to believe the impossible a second time. Bianca snatches a microphone, hurries down the steps and runs full sprint down the aisle in her high heels saying, into the microphone, "I told you! I told you! Bishop! My husband! Is risen!"

By the time Bianca is close enough, though, she hears Scoop telling them. "Naw, naw, y'all. I'm not that dude. My name is Moses. I'm his son."

Bianca's face turns crimson. She huffs and puffs, "His son?! His son?! You weren't his son Friday morning when we made love!" The people's gasp airs out the sanctuary. Bianca lunges, screaming with two hands set to strangle, but she is held back. Bianca shakes loose and runs for the altar, for the only other man who could keep on her throne as first lady. "Will! Please help me. Comfort me, Will." By the time Will gets out of his chair, Bianca is upon him, hugging him, her face crying against his chest. Ameena runs up the chancel steps, raising a denying finger. "Oh no you don't!" She pries Bianca away from Will and slaps her. "Get your hands off of my fiancé!" Bianca rubs the slapped side of her face and says, "Fiancé?" Bianca sees Ameena's ring and passes out in nearly the same spot as last week.

Ameena, with her work done here, comes away tugging her blouse, unruffling as she goes back down the altar steps. Will wears a look that asks *what just happened here?*

Bianca must've been playing possum because as soon as the pair of deacons try to assist, Bianca pops up, warning them to keep their hands to themselves. They don't listen. The deacons whisk away a hollering Bianca, to be promptly admitted into a mental facility, judging by her behavior during service, for trying to make a Jesus out of the philandering bishop, and even having relations with the dead bishop's son.

It takes the church a while to settle down and refocus; it's not everyday someone gets jack-slapped at the pulpit. When Will steps up to preach, his arms flop at his sides as if his sermon could only be anticlimactic to everything that has transpired. He waits. He feels his sermon shapeshifting by the minute. This is the week after their national tragedy; there's no way he doesn't lead with that.

Will grabs the pulpit by the handles and breathes deep. "What happened here last week, was terribly tragic. The injured are suffering and the families of the deceased are suffering the loss of their loved ones. We're all still grappling. I thank you all for showing up in such large numbers, for showing your resolve, for not letting them win –" he says, along with a few other obligatory mentions he must list, so that he leaves no one feeling left out of his considerations, but Will concludes, "… I say tragic, but also unique. This was not the work of a madman or extremist motivated by hatred, in which we couldn't even hope to comprehend. This one, we can examine up close. This one… was very unique. So, know that when I speak about this church shooting, I am not indirectly speaking about other church shootings. No. This one…" He pushes on his pulpit grip and straightens his elbows, which leans him back. "This one stands alone."

"Money was taken…" His finger wags like a windshield wiper blade. "…but it wasn't taken for greed. If you were following the news you would know that the money was dropped off at someone's doorstep. Not a dime spent. It was given to someone who needed it – someone the church turned away. So, greed was not the motivation behind three gunmen bursting through these doors. But don't mistake it for charity neither. Charity is where you give of your *self*. That money never belonged to the robbers. They didn't earn it; they simply possessed it. So, it's not charity… It's not greed…" He takes his time scanning the congregation. "…but it's something, amen? They didn't do it just so; it was planned, it was coordinated. When those men came in here and robbed this church; it was their misguided attempt to try to help someone that *we* should have helped." Will stiffens, suddenly, his right hand becomes a tomahawk hacking the pulpit on these words. "They tried to hold, us, accountable!" The power of his voice and the force that he bangs the pulpit startles his audience. He's beginning to feel the furnace in his belly, but it's too early. He has to retract. He goes in a different direction. Will says, "I have an announcement to make. The board has elected a new pastor, they've made an offer. By Monday, I expect to accept." The congregation rises to their feet with applause, while Will awaits his punchline. He lets the building get quiet before he raises a brow and says, "My only question to them is: are you sure?" He smiles as if to hide the canary is in his mouth. "We'll see if you feel the same way after this sermon. I'm going to say what needs to be said up here. Are you sure you want the truth!" They clap even more spiritedly. Will leans on the pulpit and waits for them to calm down.

And then he returns to the word. "Here's what I want you to understand. Sinners know what your role is. If we were doing our jobs, these prisons and homeless shelters would be half empty and hunger would be non-existent. Don't believe me? Huh? Think I'm crazy? Well, think about this: there are more churches in this country than federal buildings. Religion in terms of dollars and in goods and services provided by religious organizations is worth $1.2 Trillion in the U.S. Economy – when the U.S. Government runs the entire country on a budget of $3.8 trillion. So, basically, if we were all on the same page; the church should be cleaning up this country rather than just making pastors rich.

There are one hundred thousand public schools in America versus three hundred and fifty thousand churches. That's three times as many. But who is teaching our children? Why is our influence not beating out the influence of the world? The U.S. has the largest Christian population in the world, yet we're the murder capital of the world. We are failing. We are failing miserably.

What national problems that we're impacting?" Will frowns at his counting fingers, "Drug crisis, heath care crisis, border crisis? The church, as an institution, is in a bubble. Together we're almost as big as the government, yet we're sitting back and watching government fail. All the while, church members know we're not living up to our promise yet defend these pastors who live like CEOs.

This is Alabama, y'all. When Rosa Parks refused to go to the back of the bus, it was church folk just like us who said enough is enough. Right here on Alabaman soil, we ran the most effective and influential boycott of the civil rights era. We took a position. And we did something.

Right now, today, social atrocities are going on all around us right now, and the only legislation the church proposes is one that has something to do with a woman's reproductive rights? But silent on everything else! Faith based organizations haven't offered not one piece of legislation on immigration, no gun laws, no hate crime bill? no healthcare bill? No bill for the protection of unarmed citizens being gunned down by law enforcement. The public knows that life begins with conception. They simply reject us being silent on every other issue and then getting all fired up behind an abortion bill because it makes us *look like* we don't care about women, but only care about her womb. They see us, the church, as those who want life sentences for a woman terminating a pregnancy but ok with privileged young men getting only probation for rape!" Again, Will pulls back smiling, asking, "Are you sure?"

"This is the same church – the black church, in particular – that led the nation to sweeping change in the Civil Rights era. Call me crazy, but I believe we can do it again. We just have to be willing to roll up our sleeves, but first we have to fix ourselves, Amen? Ultimately, we have to do our jobs…"

Many come forward to get saved that day. Usually, they're ushered to the back where they fill out membership paperwork and schedule baptism, but this time Will has the microphone go around to those who came to be saved and to rededicate their lives.

When the microphone reaches Scoop, he can hardly fight through the tears. "My name is Moses." He says, "I just want God to use me," – and God will. His own future is being a single father to four children who are not his. He's had a good example in Big Mike who was a father to him, knowing that Scoop was not his biological child. With the resources Scoop will soon inherit, he vows to extend Mike's living legacy by starting a ministry in Mike's name, to mentor and support underprivileged children. So, using his inheritance to fund the ministry, a large portion of the money Simon tried to keep for himself, ultimately ends up in service of the people.

Ameena too comes forward to rededicate her life to Christ with her arm around Rose; the two, inseparable. After having asked God and then having her daughter's life spared, and now loosed from her past by way of forgiveness, there was no way Ameena could stay seated at altar call. When Will brings the microphone to Ameena, she says a few words, and tries to hand the microphone back to Will, but he doesn't let her off so easily. "Don't act like that," he says. "I know what God has been doing in your life. Better testify and help somebody today." Will passes hands her the microphone and steps back.

Ameena sighs and grows weary, not wanting this, but knowing in the spirit of the black church, holding back a testimony like hers is almost as bad the robbing someone of their hope, their inspiration, their blessings. They encourage Ameena like she's a child at bat in T-ball game; church mothers speak out, *take your time, baby. Alright, now.*

"Giving honor to God. I come before you, on the mend. See, I've been broken in places nobody would think to look. There's probably a lot of questions surrounding me, right now – like, why was the money brought to my house. Why was a man shot to death on my lawn just yesterday…? He was no crazed fan. No." Ameena touches the corner of each eye to blot tears. "It's a lot closer to home than that. That man had raped me when I was just twelve years old." The congregation rumbles. Ameena looks up and sees every mouth covered and every pair of eyes wide. Ameena throws an arm around Rose again. "Rose, here… Is not my sister. She is the child of that rape. The reason I moved from Manhattan back to Huntsville after all these years, is because Rose was diagnosed with cancer. Any parent who has had a long, drawn out bout with cancer knows that the medical bills can pull you down into poverty. Many of the parents end up filing for bankruptcy – I know because for the last year now, I've been talking with other parents in waiting rooms of doctors' offices. *I* myself was at that breaking point. This is right around the time when the church cut off its support. I came to the bishop personally to tell him what I was going through, asking for support, and he tried to take advantage of me when I was most vulnerable." Many women stand, suddenly – looking on as if they've discovered a twin. Ameena looks at them and says, "I know I'm not the only one… I can see you right now." They make themselves known with Amens, with holy hands raised and streaming tears. Ameena continues. "I can't tell you how upsetting it was, to watch Simon on television, in the background cheesing behind the governor when they introduced life sentence portion of the bill. I saw him in a news interview say he was compelled by God to become involved politically. Where was your God when I came to you, asking help for my daughter? And you did what you did!" Ameena fights through tears. "I'm gonna say this… This isn't my business to put out there, but it's the truth. Bishop's very own wife is a woman he met pregnant and in financial straights, which he used to leverage marriage with a woman twenty years younger, a woman who may have never married him otherwise." Ameena's microphone picks up the voice of Scoop, the bishop's newly unveiled son, who stands shoulder to shoulder with Ameena, showing that he too had been hoodwinked, by yelling out, *He took advantage of my mother!*

The logic, the scheme, suddenly comes together for Ameena. "Why do you think he changed the rules on the financial support? Think of who makes up ninety-nine percent of the people who get direct financial assistance from the church: the elderly and women with children. Once we could no longer go to the administrative office, he knew it would bring us face to face with him, where he could use what we need to get what he wants." Ameena's claim is confirmed by all the beautiful and shapely women crying out or standing in silence with their heads shaking over praying hands, now seeing the invisible net that bishop had entangled them in. There seems to be double the twelve or so that Will knows about. Ameena continues, "The way I see it: the life sentence should be applied to Criminal Domestic Violence, if anything. We, the church, do need to stand firm that abortion is wrong, but the church *also* needs to step up in *support* of women, legally, Amen?" The women stand to show support for her words. Ameena drops her head in shame. "I'm sorry, I… I didn't mean to get up here and get political… But If there is anything I've learned in this past week; I would say that the biggest disservice we can do to ourselves and to our children is to suffer in silence. Anyone dealing with a spirit of pride knows that it tricks you into thinking it's better to suffer than ask for help. See, asking for help feels to us like admitting defeat. The spirit of pride also tricks you into thinking that asking for help is also putting your secret out in the atmosphere, and suddenly you fear what people think of you." Ameena puts her hand on Rose's shoulder again, and says, "My daughter was diagnosed with cancer. Recently, they said it became terminal. She's fifteen, y'all. They gave her some medication and sent her home with me to die. You can never truly swallow that. I was devastated. I was suffering in silence. I'm so glad that this man, our new pastor, insisted on coming to my aid. I don't know what I would have done without him. Will encouraged me to ask God." Ameena remembers crying in her living room next to the money she refused to keep, where she confronted God about Rose's healing. "No one knows why God will create a miracle for some and not for others, but I do know this: if you do not take it to Him, you have already sealed your fate, Amen?" Ameena speaks with a hand smoothing back over her hair, still in disbelief of what she will announce. "Last night. Rose passed out on the floor, and we thought that her time had finally come. She was unresponsive. She was rushed to the hospital by ambulance. I had been sitting in the waiting room for what felt like an eternity before the doctor finally came out…" The congregation knows that Rose isn't dead because she's standing there, but… As Ameena pauses, it seems too calm, too unassuming to expect what she is about to tell them, as if they're waiting to hear her gratefulness for having more days, weeks, months maybe with her dying daughter. Remission – *after* a terminal diagnosis, seems a bit too much to expect. Ameena continues, "But when the doctor finally came out. He said he couldn't medically explain why Rose had passed out." Ameena still sees her audience ready to be underwhelmed by what she will say. "But spiritually, the doctor believes that, like God put Adam asleep to remove a rib out of his body, that God put Rose to sleep so He could take cancer out of her body." Praises are already going up as Ameena announces Rose's clean bill of health.

The choir sings:

> *Way maker*
> *Miracle worker*
> *Promise keeper*
> *Light in the darkness*
> *My God*
> *That is who you are*

After service, Raquel and Moses, brother and sister by blood and now also by the blood of Christ, exit the church together, getting to know one another. Will and Ameena, New Birth's new pastor and future first lady stand together while members walk up to them and speak life into their future together. Will, Ameena, and Rose, this new blessed family, are the last to leave the service.

EPILOGUE

THE place is guarded. They sit at a stone picnic table and bench, talking like spies. In Bianca's background there is a white, boxy building. In Levi's background there is a tall, wrought iron gate – a sane, functioning society bustling just outside of it. Bianca smiles. The last thing she expected was a visitor. She looks up for the first time. "You have a church?"

"Yes. Small, but… Yes."

"After what you've done? How is that possible?"

"I'm doing it ain't I? Wasn't Moses a murderer?"

Bianca trembles and then starts mumbling, partially audible, "I'm doing it again..." She wrings her hands and fades into whispers. "God... man..."

Levi reaches out across the table for her hands and just misses. Bianca folds her arms, her head down and shaking as she tries to block out the whispers. Levi says, "I love you, Bianca. I always have."

Bianca raises her index finger and stares at it with burning intensity, and with clenched teeth, she whispers hard, "There's a difference... A difference..."

"Bianca."

She looks up, confused, as if she's trying to make out the identity of the man that sits before her, and then she smiles.

"Hello Levi," she says as if they've just sat down.

He takes Bianca's pointed hand and holds it gently. "I'm going to take care of you. You can put your trust in me."

She's gone drifting again. On her meds, she has the attention span of an infant. Suddenly she straightens up, smiling nostalgically, "Did I tell you how the pastor used to come by our house? We had a small church and they used to come around to collect dues, or if you have a death in the family, the pastor would come by and sit with you. Pray with you. Well, momma... On a day she knew the pastor would come by, she'd put us all to work, cleaning the whole entire house. We'd have that house so clean you could eat off the floor. She'd make a big dinner: fried chicken, collard greens, potato salad, pecan pie. It could be a Tuesday, and we'd be dressed in our Sunday best – me and my brother and sister. When the pastor knocked on the door, before momma opened the door, she would line us all up in a row so we could all greet him unison. Good evening Pastor Dudley." Bianca gazes with her chin resting on her knuckles. "Daddy used to get jealous cause momma never made such a fuss over him. Daddy would say, 'He's a man just like me.' But momma," says Bianca "...would cut her eye and say back, 'and tell me just how many souls have you saved?'" Bianca laughed.

"How about the pastor's wife? What did she look like?" Levi had heard the story before; he knows where her buttons lie. His questions lead her on into a place of vulnerability.

"She was pure. She had the prettiest little hands..."

Levi giggles. "When you say pure, you mean fair-skinned?"

"Oh yeah. Where I come from pastors don't settle for anything less than high yellow." Bianca touches her face in fright. "They took away all my mirrors. Am I getting darker?"

Levi turns grim. "I didn't wanna say anything."

"No..." She claws Levi's hand as she spies left and right, whispering, "Get me out of here."

"So, what's your answer, Bianca? I need a first lady. You and me, we can raise our son together and be married. Will you be my first lady?"

Bianca lights up, "Be your first lady? Oh my…" But then she sinks to a dark place. Some part of her keeps rising up like a fish swimming up silvery near the surface but then sinking back into the murky depths. Bianca gathers her hands in front of her and says, "You say small church?"

Levi shrugs. "Gotta start somewhere."

Bianca raises a hand and wiggles it. "Nah. I prefer New Birth Baptist. Simon had so much dirt on the leaders and board members, he used it to get them to do his bidding. I will use all that dirt, if I have to, to make you the pastor. And get that tar baby, Ameena, off of my throne." her eyes hold a campfire blaze. Bianca squares her shoulders and says, "*I* am first lady."

About the Author

Rod Palmer was born in rural Charleston, SC, from a Gullah Geechee community where storytelling is the lifeblood of the culture. Rod now resides in Columbia, SC where he supports a handful of social causes locally and helps other writers hone their craft.

Other Titles by Rod Palmer:

Karma Wears Versace
Karma Wears Versace II: Man Eater
The Harvest: Complete Series
The Work-Husband Caper
A Pimp In The Pulpit

www.ingramcontent.com/pod-product-compliance
Lightning Source LLC
Chambersburg PA
CBHW071412100726
47908CB00004B/1147